Sign up for our newsletter to hear
about new and upcoming releases.

www.ylva-publishing.com

OTHER BOOKS BY CHEYENNE BLUE

Girl Meets Girl Series

Never-Tied Nora
(Book #1)

Not-So-Straight Sue
(Book #2; Coming 2016)

NEVER-TIED
NORA

WILL LOVE TRIUMPH
OVER FAMILY?

CHEYENNE BLUE

Ylva

ACKNOWLEDGEMENTS

All my thanks and love to the team at Ylva for helping me polish Nora and Geraldine's story. A particular shout-out to Jove, my amazing editor, and Michelle, my project manager, for their tireless work and enthusiasm.

CHAPTER 1

SHE WAS EXACTLY MY KIND of woman.

I was interested from the first moment I saw her leaning against the bar in my favorite queer club, sipping demurely on a glass of white wine. Her lush figure enticed me, and her dark hair and olive skin made me wonder if she was from warmer climes. That she was new to the London scene was obvious as she was alone, but from the glances coming her way from women on the prowl, I knew that wouldn't last long. She was at ease in the club, unlike the girl sitting alone who was obviously a nervous straight woman out for a different kind of thrill.

Ignoring the hopeful glances of the straight girl, I honed in on the dark newcomer, sweeping in with my practiced patter and casual seeming touches. "I'm Nora," I said as my fingers brushed against hers in an approximation of a handshake that lingered and caressed rather than grasped. "You're new here. Let me protect you from this mob." With a wave of my other hand, I indicated the rest of the patrons.

She smiled, and it was wicked and feline. "I'm perfectly able to look after myself," she said in delightfully accented English. "But you can entertain me however you like, Nora."

Bingo. I signaled for two more glasses of wine, picked up her hand, and pressed a kiss to the palm. "What if my intentions are less than honorable?"

"Then I would like you the better for it."

The wine arrived, and I linked my hand firmly with hers and led her off to a dark corner. Out of the corner of my eye, I could see at least a couple of other women lose interest in the face of my obvious stake. *Tough*, I thought. *They should have been quicker.*

My dark beauty slid into a booth, and I sat next to her, my thigh pressing firmly against hers. She pressed back, her movement assured, and picked up her glass. "*Salud*, dear English girl."

"I'm Irish," I corrected. "My family is from Ireland where we have clouds and cliffs that go on forever and the most beautiful women in the world."

"I'm Giovana," she said, "and I'm from Italy, where we have food and wine to make you melt. Our women are hot and fiery, and *they* can keep going forever. You can call me Gigi." Her hand explored the long line of muscle in my thigh.

I was home and hosed, as my Aussie friend, Sue, liked to say. Onto a certainty. I captured Gigi's hand and held it palm down against my leg. It was hot, even through my jeans. I thought of how her hands would skate over my body later, putting her heat to good use.

I tilted my head and let my gaze linger on her throat where her pulse beat fast and urgent. "And will I get a chance to see if I can outlast you?"

She leaned forward, and her breath feathered over my face. "Nora, I think you and I will get to do many things together. But you have to come home with me tonight to find out."

I wasn't going to argue.

"Nora…" Gigi whispered my name into my mouth as we kissed for the first time in a dark corner of the club. "Nora!" She gasped as I gently bit her nipple through her clothing. "Noraaaaa," she sighed in a dark doorway on the way to her place. And finally in bed she screamed my name loud enough to wake her flatmate and bring him crashing into the room brandishing a bedside lamp to use as a weapon, only to find me between Gigi's thighs, mouth clamped to her pussy as she came in great gulping waves of pleasure.

When Gigi finished coming, when her flatmate finished apologizing, when all three of us finished laughing, Gigi asked if her flatmate could join us. I refused point-blank, and he backed out the room, still apologizing even as his boxers clearly outlined that he wasn't sorry at all. I locked the door, and then Gigi showed me some lusty Italian loving that lasted well into the early hours.

"Stay if you want." Gigi sat up in bed, tousled and delicious. "I'm at my most…creative in the mornings, and Italian coffee is the best in the world."

For a second the idea was tempting, but I'd had enough awkward morning afters with near strangers to know it was never as good as it sounded. I mustered a smile. "I would like that very much, but I have to be at my family's place for breakfast. We Irish are early risers. I have to go." I took a last pass along her body with my lips and got out of bed. My clothes were scattered around the room, and I retrieved them as I dressed.

I kissed Gigi goodbye and deflected her hints about meeting that evening. One night with a new woman was a charm, but I wasn't looking for more. "Never-Tied Nora" my family called me. Originally a childhood joke about my inability to tie my shoelaces, but now a reference to my footloose ways and single lifestyle. So I kissed Gigi thoroughly, told her what a wonderful night it had been, and repeated with all the Irish charm I could muster that I was so sorry I had to leave.

Gigi pouted, her thick lashes downswept over her beautiful eyes. "Ah, too bad, sweet Nora. Although you didn't want Lucas to join us tonight, I was going to ask a lady friend along later."

So Gigi was as much of a player as me. Temptation and interest swam in my blood, and for a moment I wavered. But I stuck to my story. After all, this was London—there was always another woman.

Luckily, Gigi's flat was in a busy area, but even so, given that it was the early hours, I walked swiftly to the main road, where I hoped I could hail a taxi. Once there, I merged into the crowds of people spilling out of nightclubs and sauntered along at a more leisurely pace, keeping one eye out for a taxi. I wasn't worried about being alone; I was tall enough to be intimidating, and confident enough to stare down most would-be hecklers. And from experience I knew that I was fleet enough to outrun all but the fittest troublemakers.

London buzzed around me. It was nearly two in the morning, the pubs were closed, and many of the nightclubs were closing. Any taxi that appeared was snapped up before I could hail it. I was only fifteen or so minutes from my parents' house, so I could make the story I'd spun for Gigi about family breakfast a reality. I didn't have my key, but I figured I could probably wake my sister, Theresa, with some gravel against her window. It would be a fair payback for all the times she'd rung my doorbell at a similar hour to crash in my bed.

Tomorrow was Sunday. Breakfasts were legendary in my parents' house, particularly on the weekend when my mam pulled out the contents of the fridge and threw it in a frying pan. Rashers, eggs, and black pudding. Beans and tomatoes, accompanied by tea so strong a mouse could trot across it. My mouth watered, and that decided me. I hadn't had Sunday breakfast at Mam and Da's place for a while. My rackety Irish family, with their good-humored insults, bad jokes, and tough love was just the thing I wanted.

I switched direction and headed for my parents' house. The street was even busier and I had to weave my way through hordes of intoxicated people, many of whom were staggering from lamppost to lamppost, giggling and clinging on to their dates, their friends, or possibly just random strangers. Two people ahead looked familiar. A male and a female, just that little bit louder than the passersby, were weaving their way along the street in the same direction as me. As I came closer, I heard "Feck you, Dec!" and that confirmed it. It was Theresa and her twin, Declan, obviously on their way home from a night out. I grinned at my luck. That would make it easy to barge in the door with them and crash with Theresa.

I hung back watching as they lurched along, arms linked. It wasn't unusual for the twins to be out together. Both had their own friends, but usually they watched each other's back, arranged "accidental" meetings for their sibling with anyone who took their fancy, and if they weren't successful, they'd make sure the other got home safely.

I jogged up behind them, then leaped onto Declan's back and clung like a monkey with my arms around his neck and my feet around his waist.

"Feck!" Declan staggered to keep his balance and swung his arms backward, trying to hammer my ribs. Theresa's laughter must have alerted him, and he said, "Nora, you bitch. I thought you were a Flannery."

5

I dropped off his back and came up alongside him. "Love you too, brother." I punched him affectionately on the arm, and he grinned his goofy gap-toothed grin at me.

"What are you doing here?" he asked.

"It's obvious," said Theresa. "She's wearing her favorite shirt and jeans, now very rumpled. Those are her pulling clothes. The latest conquest must live nearby."

"That way." I waved in the general direction.

"She throw you out?" Theresa's little face, all sharp chin and angles, taunted me. "Not surprised. I'd evict you too."

"I left. As I always do."

"More likely she didn't want to keep you."

I thought of Gigi, her olive skin warm in the glow from the bedside light, her hair disarrayed and disheveled, the marks my mouth had left on her breasts, and the magic her lips had worked between my legs.

"Oh, she wanted to keep me all right." I grinned as I remembered her suggestion of a threesome. "Can I crash with you tonight?"

Theresa sighed in pretend reluctance. "I suppose so."

I linked arms with the two of them, and we kept walking in the direction of our parents' house. Three abreast, it was harder to avoid knocking into people, but we barreled along, letting our laughter carry us through. We turned onto a side street, where there were dark houses and fewer people.

Declan's pace slowed. "Feck it."

Theresa slowed, too, and that forced me to keep pace with them. "What is it?"

"Fergal Flannery."

"Is Young Seánie with him?" Theresa asked.

"No, it's Fergal and someone I don't recognize."

"We can take him then. Three to two—good odds."

"Hang on," I interrupted. "Count me out. I'm not fighting anyone, not even a Flannery. I just want to get home to Theresa's bed."

"If you want to crash with me, you'll stand with your family," Theresa said in a voice as sharp as her chin. "Just because you're never home anymore, you think the feud is done and dusted. It's not, Nora. It'll never be."

"I wouldn't even recognize most of the Flannerys now," I said, even as I straightened, and pushed my sleeves up away from my hands.

"Take a good look," said Theresa. "Short, pugnacious build, ginger hair, wild eyes. Look hard, for if you ever come across Young Seánie in a dark alley, he'll be hammering into you before you can say Janey Mac."

"But it's not Young Seánie. Just let it go."

"For feck's sake, you don't just let it go!" exploded Declan. "Especially not on a Saturday, the brawling night of the week."

Theresa nodded agreement and then we were on them. I could see Fergal's expression, even in the dim light, and while it wasn't mean and ugly, he wasn't about to invite us for a pint either.

"The fecking Kellys," he said. "Two of them." His gaze flickered between the twins—he obviously hadn't recognized me.

"Three," said Theresa. "Let me introduce my sister—"

"Nora," finished Fergal staring at me with an eerie intensity. "So sorry I didn't recognize you. Haven't seen you about in a long time. Been running scared?"

I glowered but remained silent, figuring there was still a chance of getting out of this with only a few insults. It wasn't that I was afraid of fighting—I'd done enough in my teen years—but it was late and I was tired. I was older, too, and this whole Kelly-Flannery feud was, quite honestly, a pain in the arse.

Fergal's friend looked uneasy. He obviously had no clue whom we were and had no truck with us. "C'mon, Ferg," he said. "There'll still be on late openers at The Panther. I'd like another pint."

For a moment, it looked as if Fergal would move on, following the promise of more beer, but then Declan swung at him. It wasn't a particularly well-timed punch, it was wild and went wide of the mark only glancing off Fergal's shoulder, but it was enough that Fergal shook off his friend's restraining hand and waded in, fists flying haphazardly.

I watched them for a minute, wondering if we needed to drag Dec out. I looked across at Theresa—she was obviously more used to this than me—and she was screaming encouragement at Dec, along the lines of "get the fecker." Fergal's friend took one look at the melee and fled, his feet thumping on the pavement. Three against one was not a fair fight, so I gripped Theresa's shirt when it looked as if she might join in, and waited. The scuffle didn't last long. A couple of punches, a lot of staggering, bluster, and bravado, and then Theresa and I dragged Declan away.

"We'll let you go this time, you poor wee thing," mocked Theresa. "You're no match for our Dec. Off you go, run home to mammy."

Fergal clenched his fist, and it looked for a moment as if he might take a swing at Theresa, but with a visible effort at calm, he turned away. "Any time you're ready, Kelly," he shot over his shoulder in Declan's direction. "Let's see if you're as brave when it's just you and me, with no sisters to hide behind."

Theresa laughed, and Fergal swung around again and lunged at her. She sidestepped, and his forward momentum carried him onward where he collided with a low wall and somersaulted into someone's front garden. To give Declan credit, he made us wait until we'd made sure Fergal hadn't broken his neck. But once his red head emerged from the laurel bush, with twigs and leaves sticking out of his hair, we left and let our laughter be the final word.

Theresa grumbled like mad but threw me a pair of Declan's pajamas and let me squash into her single bed. Her bony elbows and knees were as sharp as the rest of her, but it was still better than the floor.

"You stink," she said, as she rolled onto her side away from me and kicked back with her feet to make some space. "You could have had a shower."

"It's nearly three in the morning," I said in a reasonable tone. "The noise of the shower would have woken Mam and Da. And I don't stink."

"You do so. You stink of girl sex."

I turned on my side, facing away from her to escape the worst of her jabbing feet. "That's because I had girl sex. You should try it some time."

"No thanks. I like my lovers to have a penis attached. And don't give me a lecture about your blue strap-on. It can't possibly be the same."

I was too tired to argue, but one thing needed comment. "How do you know I have a blue one?"

"Went through your bedside drawers the last time I crashed at your flat."

"For feck's sake. Is nothing sacred?" In truth, I wasn't surprised. Theresa was insatiably curious and had quizzed me about the finer points of girl-on-girl action before. Not because she wanted to try it, but because she was nosy. It was just like her to poke through my things. "Better not leave me alone here tomorrow. I wonder what's in your bedside table?"

"You'll never know. It's locked. Mam's as bad as you." And then there was only the sound of her soft snoring.

I slept well despite Theresa's bony knees and elbows, and it was gone nine when, freshly showered, I made my way downstairs. The rest of the family was already clustered around the breakfast table—Mam and Da, my brother Brian, my sister Mary, Declan, and Theresa.

Like me, Brian had already flown the nest but he dropped around most weekends for Sunday breakfast and, I'm sure, so that Mam could do his laundry for him. So there they all were, shoveling bacon and eggs into their faces as if there were a famine.

I paused in the doorway, seeing the familiar dark heads of my brothers and sisters, Mam's pepper and salt hair, and Da's bald pate. My family. My mad, rambunctious, argumentative family. Always ready with an insult. Always up for a music session or a drinking session. Always there for me if I needed them.

"Nora, love! Theresa said you came home with her." Mam surged to her feet and over to the cooker. Food is love in our family, and Mam showed it by reheating the frying pan and pulling more rashers and eggs from the fridge.

"'Lo, sis," mumbled Brian. The mug of tea he waved in salute sloshed dangerously close to the rim.

I raided the drawer for cutlery, dragged a chair to the table, and elbowed my way in between Mary and Da.

"Still the same careful dresser, Nora." Mary smoothed the wrinkled sleeve of my shirt.

"She was thrown out very early by some girl," said Theresa. "We bumped into her around two. Poor Nora, never invited to stay all night."

"Pot. Kettle." I gave her my sweetest smile.

"Hey, that's below the belt!"

"That's enough now." Mam whirled around from the cooker with what seemed to be an instantly cooked plate of food in her hand. "Leave Nora alone. At least let her eat her breakfast in peace."

"What else will we talk about then?" Theresa's sharp little face glowed with mischief.

"We ran into Fergal Flannery last night." Declan looked up from his breakfast. "With a friend."

Da glared across the table. "I hope this story ends with you getting the better of him, and no police involved."

"It does," said Theresa. "The friend ran off, and Dec thumped Fergal good. He ended up in a laurel bush in someone's front garden. You should have seen his ugly mug emerging with half a hedge stuck in his hair."

There was a roar of laughter. I laughed too, even as I noted Theresa's slight rearrangement of events, making Dec out to be the hero.

"Nora wasn't much help though." Theresa shot me a sly look. "She reckoned we should let him be."

I glared at her. "Dibber-dobber."

"Well, that's what you said."

Da's voice was flinty and cold. "So you don't support your family, Nora? No doubt you'd let bygones be bygones, and you'd shake a Flannery by the hand and invite them along for a pint?"

"No." I shifted uncomfortably in my seat. "But this feud's been going on forever, and I don't see the point in stirring it. Surely it's time to let it go?"

Da put down his knife and fork and turned to face me. "If one of the boys said that, I'd have them out the back, son or no son. But you're my daughter, so I'll cut you a little slack. Sixty years ago, Cormac Flannery betrayed Oisín Kelly. The two of them came from the same village in Sligo where their fathers had been friends and their fathers before them. Cormac and Oisín hitchhiked to Dublin together. They got the boat to Liverpool together. They worked on the building sites together, moved from Liverpool to London together. And then Cormac Flannery took the foreman's job that should have been Oisín's, and then Cormac sacked him. That's not how mates behave. So Nora, you make a decision right now. Are you with us or against us? There's no easy midpoint here."

I was silent in the face of his vehemence. Like all my siblings, I could repeat that story word for word. It had been told to me as a scrappy wee child before I started school. It had been repeated again and again whenever the Kelly kids had a fight with the Flannery kids in the playground. And it had been drummed into us as we got older. It was the one thing that could never be overlooked. The Flannerys and the Kellys were mortal enemies.

I'd lived away from home for seven years, and in that time, I'd rarely seen a Flannery. I moved in different circles now, and London was big enough that accidental meetings were rare. The meeting with Fergal last night was the first time I'd seen a Flannery in years. I'd moved on, forgotten what I considered to be an irrelevant bit of family history, just another tale of times gone by. But, I was learning, the rest of my family didn't see it that way. Declan and Theresa last night; Da this morning. I looked over at Mary, but she was eating steadily, playing no part in the conversation.

The feud didn't seem relevant to me anymore, but family was family, and I owed it to them to stand with them.

Da waited for my answer.

"I'm a Kelly," I said. "Of course I'm with you. Young Seánie had better watch out if he crosses my path."

In the laughter that followed, Brian was the only one who remained silent.

My affirmation broke the tension, and once again there was the clatter of cutlery and the hiss of the frying pan as Mam put on more bacon to satisfy the bottomless pits that were my family. Things were back on the rails.

"That's the excitement done for the morning," complained Theresa. "There's only football and politics left to talk about."

There was a silence. Then Mary put down her mug with a thump. "I've got news if anyone's interested. I've met someone."

"You're joking," Declan mumbled around a mouthful of toast. "Who'd have you?"

Mary glared at him. "Way to go, baby brother. Do you want to hear about him or not?"

"Of course we do, love." Da patted her hand. "And as long as he's employed and treats you nice—"

"Fertile," added Theresa.

"Lives nearby," said Mam.

"Arsenal supporter." This from Brian.

"And not a Flannery," chorused Declan and myself, "then you can have him."

"His name's Liam Muldoon. He's from Kilkenny, lives in Shepherds Bush, works in insurance, and he supports Chelsea—"

A snort from Brian.

"—and I'm not putting the fertile part to the test for a while, if ever."

Mam crossed herself. Even the thought of sex for recreation not procreation had her in a tizzy.

"And he loves me." Mary—my pragmatic and practical sister—looked positively gooey-eyed.

Brian nudged me. "She's blushing."

And indeed she was. I opened my mouth to continue the teasing, but Mary looked me full in the face. "Laugh all you want," she said. "Especially you, Nora. But when love hits, and it will, it'll come with a wallop when you least expect it. You'll be in the pub, in the takeaway, locking eyes with a stranger on the tube, and there'll be strange feeling in your belly—"

"And you'll think 'I knew I shouldn't have had the Vindaloo,'" muttered Brian.

Mary ignored him. There was an intensity to her words, a conviction. It reverberated in her low voice; it shone with zealotry from her pale eyes. Her stillness made me uncomfortable, and I fidgeted in my seat before I broke eye contact to reach for the ketchup.

"—and you'll know that this is it. This is the one for you." There was a silence, and then we all started clattering the cutlery once more. But I saw Mam squeeze Mary's hand in solidarity.

Yeah, right, I thought. Love like that is for the Marys of the world—good, kind, solid, heterosexual sort of people. Not for me. And long may that last.

CHAPTER 2

THE PUB WAS DARK, ONE of those little backstreet places so dimly lit you could hardly see the level of liquid in your glass. It had cozy nooks like they have in Ireland, which are perfect for private conversation. My friend Sue and I were out for wine, a chat, and to complain about our former lovers. Sue was nursing a not-quite-broken heart; mine was more a dented ego, but we both felt the need to vent.

This particular pub was not one of our usual haunts—not the rowdy dive that Sue preferred where inked and muscled blokes strutted around the bar, and not the dyke pub with pool tables that was my favorite spot.

My bruised ego was because my friend-with-benefits had stopped returning my calls. I guessed she'd seen me leave the club with Gigi last week and had stomped off in a huff. It had happened before, but Tash and I had no arrangement past hooking up for an enjoyable few hours every so often, and in the past, I'd always been able to talk her 'round. Not this time though. We weren't "girlfriends." At least I didn't think so. Maybe, I was learning, Tash did.

Sue's boyfriend of three months, Leo, had told her he wanted to see other women. Sue was an indignant mix of anger and woe. Only the other week she'd told me it might be love.

Now her confidence was in the toes of her knee-high leather boots, and wounded pride had her spitting bullets into her red wine.

"Leo invited me to the opening of his exhibition," she said. "Tiny paper cups of cheap wine, soggy samosas, and arty types discussing the hidden symbolism in his paintings. I was his date. I thought that counted for something. I hung around in a drafty gallery talking about brushwork and the reflection of light." She snorted. "Two hours of my life I won't get back."

Last week she'd been starry eyed about his paintings and his prodigious talent with a brush—and in bed. It didn't seem fair to remind her of that.

We settled in for some deep-and-meaningful conversation, the sort that involved fixing the troubles in our lives and workplaces. Occasionally during chats like this, when we were sufficiently lubricated, we even came up with a workable solution for world peace.

I was at the bar getting the next round when *she* walked in. Medium height, curvy build, and looking damn fine in tight, dark jeans and a white gypsy shirt with lacing down the front. It was her hair that made me look twice. It was the richest auburn and fell in bouncing curls nearly to her waist in a wild, untamed cloud. Her skin was creamy and dusted with freckles, like caramel drops on milk. She paused in the doorway and looked around as if she was meeting someone. Her gaze passed over me, paused, and snapped back. For a fractured instant, our gazes met across the bar, and in a strange and wonderful moment, I saw my past and present and future in her eyes. She took a step into the room, and for a wild and glorious second, I thought she felt it too, that she was moving toward me.

I took a pace in her direction. The noise of the bar faded to a muted buzz, and the only thing that mattered was her eyes and how they made me feel. But then the barman returned and put down the wine, and his request for money was loud enough to knock me out of my trance.

As I fumbled for cash, my mystery woman waved to someone outside my line of sight and moved away to a corner. Although I looked, I couldn't see whom she was meeting. My gaze followed the hole she left in the room. A surge of lust arrowed down to my pussy, but there was something else as well. I had a curiosity about her. It wasn't just the hair, which was a wondrous thing in itself, or her intense eyes that had trapped me in their gaze. It was the way she carried herself with a quiet confidence. I wondered what her name was and where she lived. I wanted to get to know her. And too, there was a tug at the back of my mind, a blur of memory, as if she were every fantasy I'd ever had, as if hers was the shadowy face I'd seen in my head when I was still a believer in True Love. Her body was the shape I'd seen as a teenager when my fingers learned the route to my clit. She was the wisps of smoke and memory that haunted my dreams.

I realized I was clenching the glass so hard my knuckles were white. I dragged in a deep breath, returned to the nook where Sue waited, and thumped the wine glasses down on the scarred table. "I've just seen my future wife," I said to Sue. "I want to woo her, date her, and live with her. In a couple of years, I'll send you a wedding invitation."

Sue peered at me over the top of her specs. Such romantic declarations were not my usual style. She was used to me playing fast and loose with lesbians, bisexuals, the bi-curious, and even straight women when I was sufficiently tempting to pull one in for the night. Sue took a hefty gulp of wine, and then seeing my faraway expression, took an equally enormous gulp of mine. "Who?"

"Over there." I gestured toward the far end of the bar. "She went that way. She's the most beautiful woman I've ever seen."

Sue twisted around to see where I was pointing, but the crowd was thick. "Beautiful? That's okay then; you're in lust, same as usual. You'll get over it."

"No," I started to say, bursting with the need to tell Sue about my epiphany. "It's—"

But she finished her wine in big mouthfuls and stood. "I'm off. I'll leave you to your hunting."

"But I've just bought wine."

She smirked and held up her phone. "Leo texted while you were at the bar. He wants to talk, and I am so going to make him pay for what he said." She bent and kissed my cheek. "But I'm not going to waste a glass of plonk." She scooped up my wine, squeezed my shoulder, and then she was gone.

I was left alone with an empty glass and a burning need to find out more about the red-headed woman. I didn't begrudge Sue her opportunity—indeed, it allowed me to make my own pursuit. I headed back to the bar.

"Same again?" the barman asked, and I nodded. Now armed with two glasses of shiraz, I went in search of the woman who'd captured my attention so fiercely.

She was sitting in one of the high-backed booths, talking to another woman. There were papers that looked like spreadsheets covering the table, and her companion was checking a column of figures. Then she stabbed a finger at a different part of the sheet, and the two of them bent to study it. It looked like a work meeting, although why anyone would have a work meeting in a busy pub was beyond me.

I waited, propped against the bar opposite and sipped my wine. My patience was rewarded when the other woman gathered the papers, slipped them into a satchel, and slung it over her shoulder. Both women stood, hugged briefly, and the other woman left.

My beautiful redhead had been the subject of admiring glances from men and women in the bar, so I didn't waste any time. I slipped into the booth and sat opposite her. The seat was still warm. I put the second untouched wine on the table.

"My friend had to leave in a hurry," I said. "Will you share a glass of wine with me?"

She looked up, and our eyes met. There was an amused half smile on her face—clearly she was used to clumsy pickup lines. Close up, she was even more breathtaking. Her skin had a creamy clarity that was usually only brought about by clever use of Photoshop, her eyes were a deep, sea green, and that wild mane shimmered and danced. I held her gaze, wondering if she was going to respond to my invitation or—heaven forbid—if she was straight. She'd probably cut me dead if so. But then she smiled, and I knew even if she wasn't gay, she was at least prepared to consider the idea.

"That's not a very original pickup line, and your own glass is nearly empty. Do you mean for us to share the full one?"

"After you." I gestured to the glass. She picked it up and narrowed her eyes wickedly at me over the rim. The sip she took left a smear of clear lip-gloss on the edge.

When she set the glass down, I captured it and our fingers brushed in the lightest of touches. Deliberately, I set my lips to the exact place where hers had been.

She watched me drink and then took the glass from my hand before it could reach the table. Her fingers were warm against mine for the briefest moment before I relinquished the glass. She turned the glass until she could again drink from the same spot.

I tried to take a deep breath, to maintain my calm and collected image, but it was impossible. She flashed a quick glance at me through lowered lashes as she drank, and when she put down the glass, her quick smile stole what air I had left. She was definitely flirting, and I was breathing as fast as if I'd sprinted for the train.

With any other woman in this situation, I would've moved around the table, sat next to her, close enough to touch, to flirt with the brush of fingertips, close enough to rest a hand on her thigh. Close enough to let the tension build between us until there was only one possible explosive outcome. But I didn't. I stayed in my seat, my heart pounding as I watched her assess me.

Her gaze raked over me, checking out my hair pulled back in a ponytail, my pale-green T-shirt, and dark jacket. She must have liked what she saw, because she said, "I'm Ger. Short for Geraldine. Blame my Irish roots for that one."

"I'm Nora. Blame my Irish roots as well." The glass was empty. "Can I buy you another drink?" I asked. "A whole glass, all to yourself?"

Her eyes crinkled in amusement. "What will you do if I say no?"

If she had been any other woman, I would have taken that as a cue to push forward. "But you won't say no," I would have said, and I would have moved closer, picked up her hand, and made a longer skin to skin touch. But I hesitated, remembering the gut-crunch of my initial reaction. If I was right, if Geraldine was someone for more than a night of my life, then my practiced patter was out of place. If she was special, then I wanted to treat her in a way different from usual. Not as just another pickup.

"I don't know," I admitted. "I'm hoping you won't. One glass of wine, Geraldine, and then if you want me to go, I will."

"It's early. My work meeting took a lot less time than I anticipated. I'd like that, Nora. After all, wine drunk alone doesn't taste as good."

My smile was wide and unrestrained. "Same again?"

"Indeed. Red wine and conversation. It's what I like the best."

I slid out of the nook and went to the bar, returning in record time. Geraldine was sitting exactly as I'd left her. Once again, I slid in opposite so that I could see her face and watch her reactions.

There was silence for a moment. I didn't want to slip into my routine, into my chat-up lines and moves of seduction. But I found I didn't immediately know what to say. I wasn't usually at a loss for words, but I'd never been in this exact situation before. Ger, too, was silent. Maybe she was waiting for me to speak, to assess my intentions.

"I saw you walk in," I said, "and then I watched you from the bar. It was obviously a work meeting. And I thought 'what eejit has a work meeting in a busy pub?' Are you some sort of pub mystery shopper?" I smiled to highlight the humor in my words.

Geraldine grinned. "My colleague has a baby and works from home. She told me she was desperate to be somewhere where there were no rattles, pureed carrots, or nappies, so she suggested meeting here."

"And is this your usual pub?" If it was, I resolved to make it my mine as well.

"No. I only came to meet Jean. Have I walked into your local?"

"This is the first time I've come here as well. My friend, Sue, suggested it because she wanted to try the Korean

21

restaurant around the corner. But she got lucky with her ex and abandoned me."

"So I'm saving your evening?" Her eyes crinkled again, in a way that made it obvious she wasn't put out.

"You're making it, Ger. I think you've just made my week."

"Wait until I start boring you with talk of my model train collection. That's the point most people suddenly remember they have to be at their granny's for dinner."

I silently blessed Brian's geeky, anorak stage in his teens. "OO or HO gauge?"

Her suddenly frozen expression had me laughing. "I bet you didn't expect anyone to actually know something about model trains. When my older brother was about ten, he had this mad train set that ran around his bedroom and out onto the landing. The track was on a ledge at head height, and he used to love booby-trapping people as they came up the stairs. He'd line up one of the engines and then accelerate it so that it was going too fast to make the corner by the hot press. It would shoot off the rails and hit them on the side of the head."

Ger nodded. "It's all great fun until someone loses an eye."

"That didn't happen. But there were a few close calls."

"Does he still have it?"

"He's nearly thirty now and his tastes have finally matured. His new obsession is Arsenal Football Club."

"Is that yours too?"

I shrugged. "I guess. Tennis is more my sport."

She leaned forward, and her fingers lightly tapped the back of my hand. "If I had any doubts at all—which I don't—that you're trying to pick me up, that was the cincher. Do you watch for the shot making and the thrill of the game, or because of the fit women in short dresses?"

"The former of course." I made my voice dignified. "I appreciate the finer points of a one-handed backhand, the smooth arc and power of an effortless serve, and the grace and beauty of Maria Sharapova's endlessly long legs."

"Hmmm." Ger considered, her head on one side and that wild hair spilling over her face. She flicked it back. "Personally speaking, I think the game was the poorer when Amelie Mauresmo retired."

"Martina Navratilova."

"Casey Dellacqua's still playing."

If I'd still had the slightest doubt that Ger was into women, it was dispelled by the listing of the out tennis players in the game.

"Sue and I went to Wimbledon last year. She was determined to get Roger Federer's autograph. At Wimbledon, the players walk around surrounded by this sort of security posse, which makes it hard to get close to them. So Sue wore these ridiculous high heels—and if you knew Sue, you'd realize she is totally not a high heel person. She complained and whined all day as she tottered around on those things. But then Federer came out with his security mob, and she rushed up to him along with about a hundred other people. She pretended to trip and went crashing through the security goons, arms flailing, and landed practically in Federer's arms."

"What did he do?"

"To give him credit, he didn't sidestep or push her away. He caught her and set her back on those ridiculous heels. Sue was so starstruck, she didn't ask for an autograph, but then the security person grabbed her arm and tried to pull her away. So she lunged forward, and gave Fed a huge smackeroo right on the lips. She was then pushed unceremoniously to one side by the security goons, but she didn't care. Made her Wimbledon."

"She sounds like a hoot, your friend."

"She's Australian. Must be something in the water down there. They're all barking mad."

There was a pause, during which Ger and I both sipped from our glasses. My heart pounded as if I'd faced off with Sharapova over three sets, and I'd barely touched my wine. Now that was unusual.

"What about you, Nora? Who would you like to kiss?"

Oh God. Right now, with Geraldine looking at me from across the table, lips slightly parted, hair wild and untamed around her face, there was only one answer. My mind spun away, and I imagined pressing my lips to hers, feeling the full curve of them soften and part under my own. But to speak the truth, to say that right now there was only one person in the world I wanted to kiss... Would I scare her away? But the way she was looking at me, her eyes luminous in the dim lighting, a trace of red wine in the corner of her mouth, urged me on.

"You, Geraldine. You're the only person I want to kiss."

She was silent, and the pub noise swelled around us—the clink of glasses, the braying laugh of a Hooray Henry, the slam of the door as someone entered or left. Her silence stretched long enough for me to worry I'd offended her, that somehow against all my gaydar and common sense, I'd read this wrong. But then she smiled, and there was that light touch on the back of my hand again.

"Keep a hold on that thought."

Daringly, I picked up her hand, turned it over, and traced a figure eight on her palm. My touch was light, but she inhaled shakily, and her hand twitched in mine.

"I'm working on it." My fingertip made another figure eight. It was also the infinity sign, I remembered, and for a second, I wondered if that was prophecy or coincidence.

Our gazes met, and her expression was open, vulnerable, and slightly wistful. Guard down, eyes wide and anticipatory with what I hoped was the promise of us. Then her expression turned warm. "Keep working on it. I'm looking forward to the results."

My resolution to take this slow wavered, and I cursed the table between us. All of a sudden the pub was too loud, the distance between us too great. More distraction was needed. "Are you hungry? Sue and I had a booking at the Korean BBQ place around the corner."

"My stomach is flapping. I skipped lunch."

I stood and held out a hand to her, and was rewarded by her soft palm in mine. "Then let's go."

CHAPTER 3

The Korean place was modern—tiled, cold, and echoey, but I didn't care. We were shown to a table at the back where huge potted plants muted the worst of the noise. It was far enough from the kitchen that the service was beyond woeful, but I didn't care. I sat opposite Ger once again and watched her expressions and gestures—the quick smile that lit her face like lightning over the ocean, and her small, white fingers with their short, blunt nails as they pointed to a menu selection.

We ate sizzling beef brought by blank-faced waiters, and if I'd been with Sue I'd have been whining about the price of everything and how that should at least get us a smile. But with Ger, complaining didn't cross my mind. Indeed, I welcomed the awful service as it meant more uninterrupted time to look, to flirt, to touch her hand, to dream, to imagine, and to fantasize about an outcome between us. We finished the bottle of wine but didn't order another. Instead, we drank water, and played the getting to know you guessing game.

"You're a professional women's hockey player," I said. "Or a coal miner. Final answer."

Her sigh was theatrical. "You've caught me. Want an autograph? Actually, my sister plays hockey. She says I should learn—I might meet someone. She reckons she's the only straight woman on the team."

I picked up her hand again. "Tell her you've already met someone."

Her gaze clung to mine. "I might do that. Or I might let her set me up with Big Betsie, the goalie. I love a woman with muscles."

I pushed up the sleeve of my jacket to show my forearm. "I have muscles," I said in pretend affront. "All the typing I do, how could I not?"

"You're a writer," she guessed. "You ghostwrite autobiographies of the rich and famous. Or you're a PhD student, four years into the world's longest thesis."

"I wish. Think dull. Think of the jobs that send you to sleep."

"Hypnotherapist? Is that how you're so successful with women?"

"You don't know that I'm successful. I could be Never-Laid Nora, the unloved."

Her expression sobered, and she shuffled her chair around the tiny table so that she was next to me. She was so close I could smell the spices from the meal on her breath. She moved her chair enough that it was angled toward mine, her legs capturing one of mine between them.

"Nora, look at me." The laughter fled her voice. "If you are the unloved, if you are the unlaid, then—"

"Then what?" I was trapped. Caught in the intensity of her eyes and the steel of her thighs.

"It's my lucky day, as you must be desperate." Warmth radiated from her fleeting smile.

She leaned forward, enough that I could see the dark flecks in her sea-green eyes. "I won't lie to you, Nora. I've gone home with women I've just met. Met them in a club, or a pub, or at my sister's hockey game. And I've spent a night with them, and at the time it was wonderful. Sex, out of this world. But afterwards? Not so much." She dragged a deep breath, sat back, and took a gulp from her water glass. "I'm tempted. I'm tempted to lean in and kiss you. Learn your taste, the sigh of your breath. See if your hair is as soft as it looks. I want to know you. Learn what your skin feels like. And in the morning we'd have coffee, and kiss, and swap phone numbers, and then I'd leave, or you'd leave, depending on where we were, and I'd wait for your call. Or maybe I wouldn't. Maybe I'd have written you off as just another one of those women, and I'd go into work, and maybe I'd cry on my boss's shoulder over you. Maybe not."

Her quiet words held me spellbound, and even the tardy waiter arriving to clear away the dirty dishes didn't interrupt.

"What do you want from me, Nora?"

My voice was a croak worthy of any frog princess. "Everything. I want everything you'll give me."

"Now? Tonight?"

Her words were a siren's song, sucking me in with long sea-fingers. They entwined in my mind, seductive, alluring, enticing. My pussy twitched, and the ache in my belly wouldn't be subdued. I wanted her. Wanted her badly. But still, there in my mind was the thought that Ger was different. She was no Gigi or Tash, a woman to be enjoyed and then forgotten. Ger was… Maybe, Ger was forever.

She was still waiting on my answer. "Yes, now, tonight. But not tonight." I pushed my hand into my pulled back hair. "It's time we left. We'll walk out of here, into the street. And we'll walk. We'll move through London together until our paths diverge, and you go home to your place and I go to mine. At that parting place, we'll stop. Maybe there'll be a quiet dark doorway, maybe not. But then, Ger, I'll take you in my arms and pull you close. There's no stars to be seen in London, but they're there all the same, above us, behind our eyes. I'll kiss you. I'll learn how you taste, the tickle of your hair, how you feel under my hands. We'll kiss, and then I'll go. Not because I don't want you—I do, so very badly—but because for us, I think, it could be more than a night. You and me. Me and you. A couple. Does that sound possible to you?"

She nodded. Her gaze was on my face, her whole attention focused on me. It was as if there were no restaurant patrons, no buzz of chatter around us. So I continued, weaving the words into a spell that I hoped would mean as much to her as it did to me.

"What happens tonight then?" she asked.

"I'll go home—alone. But tomorrow we'll meet again and continue this. Is that what you want, Geraldine?"

She nodded once more, and in the half light, I again felt that tug of knowledge. Her profile, her face, her hair. A tickle of memory somewhere in my mind. Was it only that she was a fantasy woman come to life? But I didn't stop to analyze it— right then, I had more important things to do.

"Tomorrow," she said. "Same place, same time."

It was my turn to nod.

We succeeded in attracting the attention of the lazy waiter, paid the bill, and left. I took her hand as we walked along the street. London was never quiet, but during that short walk, it was as if we were alone. It was me and her and how our skin touched and our arms brushed. We came to a major intersection, and she paused. "I go left here."

"And I go right."

There hadn't been that darkened doorway, there hadn't been a stolen kiss. There was a coiled tension about her, and I sensed she was waiting for me to make the first move. London swirled around us, busy even at that hour on a weekday. Traffic rumbled past, pedestrians parted around our immobile figures with barely a glance. It was as public a place as I could imagine. But I wasn't letting her go without some sort of promise. The pulse of anticipation beat strongly.

I tugged on her hand, bringing her closer to my body, and she half turned so that she faced me. My arm wrapped around her shoulder; hers pushed underneath my jacket to settle around my waist. Her hands warmed my skin through the shirt. Her lips parted slightly, a half smile on her face.

The evening had been building to this one shining moment.

I pushed my free hand into her hair, feeling its luxuriant weight. Her breath puffed on my face, and then I kissed her. The lights turned red, amber, green, amber, and back to red again as we kissed. I was tentative at first, my lips barely tasting hers, but Ger was having none of it. Her hands tightened on my waist, and she closed the space between us. Her breath was spicy with ginger and garlic from dinner, but I didn't care, and besides, mine would have been the same. What mattered was that she was in my arms, and the tango beat of my heart urged me forward.

A swift moment to draw breath and then my lips claimed hers, softly, then forcefully as she yielded underneath me. My head spun from her closeness, and right then I wanted nothing more than to move the kiss forward and take her home.

But this was about more than tonight. I eased away, and her hands fell from my waist.

"Tomorrow. I'll see you then."

"Tomorrow." She swung away through the crowded streets, her hair subdued under the street lights. I watched until I couldn't see her anymore, and then I turned the other way toward my flat.

I wanted to talk about the evening, and I thought about calling Sue, but then I remembered she was with Leo, no doubt getting shagged each way to Sunday. So instead, I walked on until I was back at my apartment.

I didn't want another glass of wine. I wanted to think about what had happened, about Geraldine, and—most of all—about my instant reaction to her. I was used to instant lust, but this feeling was new to me. When I met a woman and fell in lust with her, my thoughts immediately spun to the bedroom. How I would kiss her, what her breasts would look like, and how she'd sound as my fingers coaxed her into a climax. What her tongue would do between my legs. All very physical things, all very immediate, and all about gratification.

While I still had the familiar deep ache in the pit of my belly, and I definitely wanted Ger in my bed, the thoughts that played in my head were a gentler, less physical kind. I imagined the two of us having coffee on a frosty morning, enjoying quiet nights watching TV, spending a night in a country B&B, and wandering around some of London's markets. I imagined life, everyday life, not just sex and satisfaction in bed. Deliberately, I substituted the Ger in my head with Gigi, but the image wouldn't fit, I couldn't shoehorn her in.

It was a strange feeling. For a moment, I even imagined taking Ger home to meet my family, but my brain spun away from that thought. My family can be overwhelming, and I didn't want to scare her away.

I was too wired to sleep, so in the spirit of optimism, I tidied the bombsite that was my flat. A quick pass with the vacuum, then I removed all traces of my friend-with-benefits and changed the sheets on the bed. I swapped the trashy novels on the bedside table for something literary, and cleaned the shower. I ignored the noisy protests of Tomás, my cat, while I changed his blanket and shook the cat hairs out the window. I even cleaned the litter tray.

I wasn't normally this much of a neatnik when I was hoping to bring someone home, but I didn't want my mess to scare Ger away before I'd worked out what it was that drew me to her. I wanted to curl up on my battered sofa in front of my gas fire with her in my arms and that glorious hair tickling my nose. I wanted conversation and intimacy. I imagined Sue's hoot of laughter if she heard me say I wanted to talk with a beautiful woman instead of fuck her. If I told Sue I was dreaming about Ger and Ger had all her clothes on in the dream, Sue would call for an ambulance. But this feeling was a heady mix of lust and what I'd felt when I first met Sue—warmth, connection and liking. I'd *liked* Sue the first moment we were introduced at work. And that instant appeal on a friendship level was also there with Ger. But unlike with Sue, who was the most platonic of friends, with Ger the like intermingled with a gut-crunching lust. Plus we both had Irish backgrounds. I saw us curled together on my sofa, swapping stories of our mad families and their traditions and expectations.

CHAPTER 4

I WAS AT THE PUB by six twenty the next evening. I'd told my boss I had a migraine coming on, and left early. If anyone noticed I'd changed into jeans and a black shirt in the toilet and left my work suit hanging over the back of my chair, they didn't say anything.

Ger arrived five minutes late. It was drizzling outside and moisture beaded on her hair in a fine mist. I was unaccountably nervous, wondering how I should greet her. I remembered our kiss of the night before, but I didn't want to overwhelm her so I settled for a smile and an offer of a drink. Ger was dressed in the same tight jeans, but this time it was topped with a loose fawn blouse. She didn't need extra adornment; her hair was enough.

I brought the red wine back to the table and slid onto the bench next to her. Ger sat with her back to the corner, one leg cocked upon the seat. Her posture was both an invitation and a barrier.

"So," she said, amused. "Here we are again then."

"Here we are."

I studied her, but I was cataloging my own response as well, checking that my reaction of yesterday wasn't purely due to wine. I took a deep breath and caught the faint scent of vanilla, and my stomach leaped in a wild way. Lust, desire, attraction, liking. It was all there, I hadn't imagined it. I'm not one for going all incense and tarot, but there was a bond between us. It was still there for me, and while last night I thought Ger felt it too, right now her expression gave nothing away.

"I was thinking about you this morning," she said.

"Can't have been too bad as you still came." I fiddled with my wine glass so that my hands wouldn't reach for her, wouldn't smooth the crease of denim over her knee where her leg was bent.

"I did," she agreed. "Last night was great, but I've been wondering what your agenda is?"

I hesitated before answering. I could respond that she was a beautiful woman and I wanted to know her better—but that was a trite reply, and one she doubtlessly heard all the time. I could say she reminded me of someone I knew long ago growing up as kids in the large, loosely aligned Irish community—but if that were true, I was sure I would have remembered her. It would also have steered the conversation down the path of "Our family came from Sligo, what about yours? Do you know Bridie McNally?" and that got old quickly. Or I could tell her the truth, as fanciful as it would sound.

"I saw you last night." I said. "It was one of those lightning moments. Yes, you're beautiful, you must know that, but it was something more."

She was silent, but it was an intent silence, not an amused or mocking one. It was her stillness that encouraged me to continue.

"I told my friend I wanted to marry you." I met her gaze—defiant, a little bit scared. Talk about putting myself out there. I half expected her to pick up her bag, drain her wine, and say "It was nice knowing you, but goodbye. And don't even consider stalking me or I'll call the police."

But she didn't. Her body tensed with a sort of vibration to it, although she was perfectly still. "Go on," she said.

I shrugged. "I must sound mad. I've never said that about anyone before. I want you to know it's not just lust. I want to find out what we can be together."

She bit her lip. The dim light of the bar emphasized her cheekbones and the high winged arch of her brows. Then she shifted her posture, lowered her leg to the floor, and moved closer to me.

"Maybe I want a friend, not a girlfriend." She tilted her head and regarded me quizzically.

One part of my mind wondered at her withdrawal. Last night hadn't been about being friends. Last night had been a step on the way to becoming lovers. But I was in too deep to draw back now. "We can be friends if that's what you want." Mentally, I added "first" to the end of the sentence. "I was thinking about you when I got home, and in at least half of those thoughts, you had your clothes on."

She didn't react and worry zigged through my chest. What had gone wrong since yesterday?

Ger studied me, eyes fixed on my face, a slight crease between her brows. "Maybe I do just want a friend, Nora."

It was the way she said it, low, slightly defeated. The voice of someone who'd been hurt in the past. I'd heard the same tone in past conquests, when they suggested dating, a commitment between us. Then, I'd been thinking how I could wriggle out of it, stay as carefree Nora. Now, there was an ache in my chest for Ger and whatever—whoever—had hurt her.

My fingers reached out and touched her mane of hair, the lightest of caresses. "I can be your friend. I mean it." And in that moment, I did. "I'm a fierce friend. Ask Sue."

Ger seemed to be measuring my words, weighing up my answers, judging my sincerity.

Her fingers picked the seam of her jeans, and she directed her words to her knees. "You must think I'm messing with you. Last night, you were coming on strong to me and I was with you all the way. Leading you on. Telling you about my past women. Kissing you. And tonight, I'm playing hard to get. At least, I imagine that's how you see it."

I was silent. To fill the space with words would be too pushy. I had to trust Ger, trust she had her reasons for this.

"I meant everything I said and did last night." She looked up, and directed her words over my shoulder to the wall behind. There was no evasion or coyness in her face. She was sincere, I felt that strongly. But something was not right. "I fall for the wrong ones," she continued. "I'm sick of getting my heart stomped on. I fall for people who see my looks and my hair, and yeah, wonder if I'm really a ginger. I need to toughen up. Or I need a friend. Preferably both." I was caught in her clear, direct gaze as she switched her gaze to my face with laser-intensity. "Which are you, Nora? Someone who's going to toughen me up by breaking my heart again, or someone who's going to comfort me as a friend?"

I couldn't answer. Anything I had wanted to say sounded trite and glib, a rehearsed patter to entice her into my arms.

Ger's expression hardened in the silence. "So all those pretty words last night about wanting to see what we could be together were just a way of getting me to bed." Her posture stiffened, and she picked up her bag from the floor.

She was leaving. Panic unlocked my throat. "No...yes... Oh *feck it*." I took a moment to gather my thoughts and tried to let the words come from a secret, deep place within me. A place from where words seldom came, as it was the inner Nora, the one that not many people saw. "I'm sorry. I'm not very good at this. I won't lie to you; I've broken hearts in the past. And I do want you in my bed. But it's not just a sex thing. It's a relationship thing. Or it could be. If you'll let it."

"And then it's a heartbreak thing." Ger said it as a statement, her voice all nuggety and hard.

"How can I say I won't break your heart? It's not a promise I—or anyone—can give. But I'm sitting here, now, with my hand on my heart, saying I don't want to hurt you. I don't want a single night with you. I want more. If you'll let me try.

"I thought you wanted that too. Did I read you wrong? If so, I'll back off and be friends, as you're asking. We can take this as slow as you like." I glanced at her face, trying to read if my words were reaching her, but her face was expressionless.

"I don't mean to sound flippant or uncaring, but this is hard for me too. You said you'd had one night stands, casual affairs. Well, so have I, Ger. My dating CV is a long string of them. So I'm not used to negotiating a relationship, and I don't know what I can say to reassure you. More likely, anything I say will have you heading for the hills. And I'm not used to talking about my feelings, or telling someone I care, that I want them to stay around. The words are hard for me to say."

She was listening to me now, her gaze intent on my face, her breathing so shallow that the rise and fall of her breasts were almost impossible to discern.

I picked up her hand. "Tell me what you want. Maybe it will be easier for me to answer."

Her gaze switched to the table, she withdrew her hand from my clasp, picked up her glass and sipped. The silence stretched, long enough that I started to worry that somehow I'd said the wrong thing, that any chance I may have had with her was over before it had started. She cupped her glass with both hands, staring down into the depths as if she could scry the future in the ruby liquid.

"While I was at university, I met the girl I thought I'd be with forever. We had adjoining rooms in the same hall of residence, and it wasn't long before we were the best of friends. We did everything together—not just classes and socializing, but cooking meals, studying, even our laundry. She'd had girlfriends before, but she was my first girl. In our second year, we moved out of hall and got a flat together. We became even more entwined—got a cat and a joint bank account. The sex was fantastic, but it was the intimacy of it all that I loved the most. Having someone who knew how many sugars I took in my tea, who'd know when my neck ached without me having to say anything. She even got on well with my family. We talked about life after uni—where we'd live, what sort of flat we'd buy, how we'd take it in turns to work and support the other so we could both get our PhDs." She paused to take another sip of wine.

"What happened?" My voice was quiet. I didn't want to break the flow of her words.

"She was studying geology, and she got an opportunity with the Colorado School of Mines. It was a fantastic chance for her. At first, we thought we'd both go, but we soon found that it was next to impossible to get a green card for me. America didn't recognize lesbian couples then, so I couldn't get any sort of spouse visa, and a not-quite-qualified architect wasn't on their wanted list. I went over on a tourist visa for three months, returned home, and moved back to live with my parents to save money for another trip. But I was trying to cram my studies in with working a bar job to earn money. I made a second trip to Colorado, but already I could tell she was looking past me, assimilating into America and leaving me behind. I'm sure you can guess what happened. Eva stayed in the States, I stayed in Britain. The long distance thing petered out. She didn't want to come back, and I couldn't live there.

"She broke my heart—not all at once in a loud crash, but in a slow peeling away of the pieces until there was nothing left. It took me a long time to get over that.

"When I was ready to start dating again, I realized how lucky I'd been the first time around. I couldn't find anyone who came close to matching what I'd had with Eva. I had a string of short relationships. I tried leaping into bed with them and hoping it would turn into more. I tried holding off and getting the friendship happening before sex came into it. Neither worked. It would peter out, or I'd leave. Or they would. So then I hooked up with women just for sex, with no expectations of more. I'm not putting anyone down if it works for them, but it didn't work for *me*."

She paused to sip her wine, and I thought about her words. There was a twist of envy working its way through me for the unknown Eva who'd had Ger and lost her. But Ger's words and description of her previous relationship echoed my own thoughts of last night. They painted the warm and comfortable relationship I'd been imagining. Not just a sexual one.

"So you see, Nora, now I don't know what to expect from you. I really enjoyed last night, and I was oh so tempted to go home with you, but that's been an unsatisfying road in the past. You say you want more from me... Well, I've heard that before too, and it's been just a line. I don't know what to say. I know there's no guarantee, but I'm scared of trying. But what I had with Eva—that type of love—well, that's what I'm looking for. What, I guess, I've always been looking for."

She raised her eyes again, and the expression in them made me catch my breath. Wariness, vulnerability, but a tender veil of hope. At that moment, I just wanted to take her in my arms, hold her, protect her, be the strong one.

She'd laid herself open for me. The least I could do was try the same for her.

I thought of what to say, how I could convince her, but when filtered as words designed to persuade, the words in my head sounded stilted and insincere. I swallowed hard. Ger had been honest. She'd told me why she was pulling back, given me her history, and laid out what she was hoping for in a relationship. Any other woman, any other time, and I would have laughed and told them to lighten up—you don't set the cage before you've trapped the monkey. I was as nervous as when I'd taken my driving test—right before I'd put my foot on the accelerator, instead of the brake, and smashed into the back of a shiny BMW. I hoped that wasn't a portent for what might happen next.

"You're way ahead of me in this, Ger. You've been in love, you've lived with someone, had a good relationship, even if it didn't end well. I've never had any of those, so I've got nothing to compare this with. Even this conversation is new ground for me." I clasped my hands together tightly to stop the tremor. "If you want us to be friends first, then that's what we'll be. If you want to take this slow—hand-holding and kissing—then we'll take this as slow as a Victorian romance. I don't want to get this wrong. But I want you to be very sure that what I felt for you last night wasn't simply a friendship thing." I dragged in a deep breath. "My sister's in love. She announced it to the whole family at breakfast. She told us it happened in an instant. She met her partner, and she just knew that he was the one for her. I laughed at the time because it sounded so unreal, like something that happens to Meg Ryan in a rom-com, not to people like my ratbag family. But she was very serious. And she told me someday it would happen to me. Of course I didn't believe her. Why would I? It flew in the face of everything I am."

I looked at Ger, at her still body and expressionless face. But her eyes gave her away, flicking over my face, absorbing every nuance of expression. She was listening to me, really listening.

"But my sister believes there's this moment of knowing, when you meet the person who will be everything to you. When she said it would happen to me, inwardly I scoffed. But now... Now, I think I believe in that moment of knowing too. Now I think it's happened to me."

CHAPTER 5

IT WAS AS IF THERE was a bubble of silence round us. Somewhere, far away it seemed, was the noise of a busy pub, a buzz of chatter, a clink of glass, but we were cocooned in our own space—me, her, this table, the here and now. The pub, the crowd, everything and everyone around us were unimportant. I'd said all I could, if she didn't believe me now, I had nothing left to convince her. If she walked away from me, I'd follow, but I thought that if she didn't take a chance on us now, it would never happen.

Then Ger picked up my hand. "And I thought I was being the fanciful one."

Joy bubbled in my chest, relief sang sweetly in my blood. I half turned toward her, picked up a curl of that gleaming hair and wound it around my finger. "You've knotted me tight, Ger. Trapped me in the work of a moment."

We were silent, our eyes taking in every aspect of the other. Our other hands found each other, touched, clasped, and we sat there, separate in our happiness, but somehow it was a shared one too.

Ger stirred first, detangled our hands, and picked up her glass. The red wine was vivid in her hand, a splash of color against the background of her light shirt. "Is this where I ask you to tell me about yourself?" Her smile acknowledged the upside-down approach we'd taken.

"I think you know me better than anyone already." I smiled, even as I examined my heart to see how it felt. I'd never been so open with anyone before, so raw, so exposed. I'd expected to feel vulnerable, uneasy, but instead there was a deep contentment, a feeling of rightness to our interactions.

So we talked about inconsequential things, as if now that the heavy words were said we hadn't room for more. We skittered over subjects, alighting briefly, moving on, and there was laughter and there was teasing. We talked over another glass of wine, and then we left the pub to have dinner. I picked up her hand in the street, and she curled her fingers around mine. I stole a sideways glance, to find her looking back at me with a soft smile. I settled her hand more firmly in mine, and we continued down the street. We agreed on an Indian restaurant and found a quiet table where we could continue our conversation uninterrupted.

We talked freely over dinner, and I soaked up every little nugget of information she dropped about herself. Any other woman, any other time, and I would have kept it superficial— after all, what did I care about the minutiae of someone's life if I was never going to see her again? But when Ger talked about her studio flat, I asked her to describe it to me, and found myself picturing the tiny balcony she mentioned, with the great view over London, her collection of deliberately mismatched plates, and the bright walls she'd painted herself, in defiance of her landlord who'd insisted on white.

"When I told him I wanted to paint two walls burnt umber, and two walls pale yellow, he was horrified. But I did it anyway, and invited him up to look. He came up with a can of matt white, that he'd intended leaving with me, but once he saw the studio, he was okay. Then when the girl in the flat below moved out, he paid me to paint the vacant flat the same as mine."

Ger had already said she'd studied architecture, so I wasn't surprised she had an eye for design and color. I thought of my own flat, which was a long way from homely and light years from stylish, and was more of a bachelor crash pad. I'd never cared much what it looked like. To me, it was a place to sleep, or for the occasional evening in when I was too broke to go out. I wondered what she'd make of it.

"Are you an architect now?" I asked.

"I'm a junior architect in a small firm. There's only three of us, plus the admin staff. The partners are husband and wife, and they're lovely. They treat me like family and, professionally, I'm learning a lot."

"What about your own family?"

"They're all mad. Irish Catholics, three generations out of Ireland, but still more Irish than anything. Guinness-drinking, hurley-playing, step-dancing, fiddle-playing redheads, the lot of us."

"Sounds like mine. Especially the mad part." The more we talked, the more the warmth and rightness of *us* expanded in my chest. London had a huge Irish community, but I'd never before been with an Irish girl. There was no particular reason for that, but now that I was, the familiarity of our similar backgrounds was another great thing.

Ger leaned over the table toward me. "*An bhfuil gaeilge agat?*"

She'd asked if I spoke Gaelic. I grinned. "*Ranganna gaeilach gach Sathairn.*"

Her expression had the same grimace of horror that any of my brothers and sisters had worn when we were dragged along to our Saturday Gaelic classes. Two hours of torment each week learning what was, to us, an utterly incomprehensible language. I switched to English. Truth was, I didn't speak Gaelic often enough to find it easy. "I'm glad I have the Gaelic though, even though I seldom speak it. It's part of my heritage, who I am. That's important to me."

She nodded. "It's handy too if you don't want eavesdroppers to know what you're talking about."

The food came at that moment, and so conversation paused as we served ourselves with chicken korma and lamb saag.

"Your turn," Ger said. "Tell me where you live, what you do for a crust."

So I told her about my flat on the top floor of a crumbling Victorian house, where the décor was eggshell white and had probably been so for about ten years. "I don't have much taste." Ruefully, I gestured to my plain black shirt and jeans and short hair pulled back in a severe ponytail. "My flat to me is a place to eat, sleep, and watch TV or read a book. But I do like to cook and have friends around for dinner sometimes. And of course there's Tomás who lives with me."

"Tomás?" Her expression was amused. I knew she didn't think for a second I had a boyfriend hiding around the corner.

"My very large, very fluffy, very affectionate ginger cat. I found him outside the house one evening when I came home. He hung around, mewing constantly, and looked pretty scrawny. He was still there the next morning when I left for work, and again that evening. So I brought him some milk and a tin of tuna. I did that for a few days, and then one evening he ran in the door with me, and followed me up to my flat. He's been there ever since. I did put posters up to try and find his owner but no one ever claimed him."

"I love cats. Eva and I had a little tabby. I miss her—she was given to Eva's parents when we split."

"You'll love Tomás. He's got this thick, ginger pelt." I reached over and twisted a wayward curl around my finger. "I've always had a thing for redheads."

Her hand came up and pressed my fingers to her cheek. "I've got a thing about brunettes with long, lean figures. Everything I'm not."

My fork clattered to the plate, and the moment hung in a bubble of space-time as I stared at her. Her eyes were huge in the subdued lighting and the expression in them took my breath—longing, needing, lust. I wanted to forget the rest of the meal and take her home, walk with her through busy streets, her hand in mine, until we came to her door—nearer than my place from what she'd said. I wanted to kiss her in the stairwell, feel the press of her hips against my own, learn her taste again, remember how she felt under my hands.

Our gazes met and clung. Her throat moved as she swallowed. "Nora. I want—"

I never did find out what she wanted as the waiter picked that moment to ask if everything was all right with our meal. The spell was broken. I smiled, told the hovering waiter the food was wonderful, and picked up my fork to continue eating. But the food could have been a tin of Tomás's cat food for all the notice I took. Ger was opposite me, and she filled my vision, consuming my thoughts until my stomach was so full with butterflies of anticipation that there was no more room for food.

Ger too seemed to have lost her appetite. "What do you do for work?" she asked, seemingly with an effort.

I glossed over my rather dull job as a paralegal and instead told her a little more about my own insane Irish family, three

46

generations out of Ireland who could probably put hers to shame. But I didn't want to talk about my family; I wanted to talk about Ger. I wanted to push my fingers into her hair and kiss her cheek, her forehead, her lips. I wanted to lie with her. Somehow we finished the meal, and even ordered dessert. The anticipation was building to a fine point of desire that needled low in my belly. It was a living, glowing thing, a flame of want that burned as fiercely as I'd ever known. Ger must have felt it too. Our touches grew more frequent—light caresses across the table, my fingers drummed lightly on the fine skin on the inside of her wrist. I brushed her cheek as I tucked a strand of hair behind her ear. And throughout it all was the knowledge that this was her and me, together. Together for more than tonight. We could draw this delicious flirting out longer, another night or two, but the day would come when we would be lovers. Despite her talk of being just friends, I knew that wouldn't be enough for us.

It was raining again as we left the restaurant, that insidious London drizzle that looks like nothing but gets you soaked.

She turned to me. "What now?"

I knew what I wanted and thought Ger wanted the same thing. The attraction between us burned fierce and bright. But after all that she'd said in the pub about heartbreak and friendship, I didn't want to push her.

"I know what I'd like." I picked up her hand and slotted my fingers through hers. "But maybe we should go home. You to your flat, me to poor, lonely Tomás."

She closed the gap between us. "What if I don't want that? What if I want you to come home with me?"

My heart skipped in my chest. Was this a test? "No. Friendship. Remember? I'm not here to—"

But my fumbling words were stopped as she lifted our linked hands, removed her fingers, and pressed her lips to my palm. Desire, fierce, and urgent, flared in a hot line connecting my palm to my breasts. My nipples tightened, and it was all I could do not to seize her and put those lips to more delectable uses.

"I don't want to hurt you, Ger. I'll see you tomorrow and we can—"

"Have breakfast."

Her eyes were wide and clear of guile. She wasn't making this easy for me.

"Breakfast?"

"Coffee then. Whatever you normally have first thing in the morning when you wake."

Her words painted a picture in my head of sunlight and two people companionably drinking coffee and making plans for dinner.

"This isn't a test of your worthiness, Nora. You've already passed that with your honesty this evening."

Still, I had to be sure. "What if I break your heart? What if it doesn't work out?"

She shrugged. "For all my fine words, there's no guarantee in life when it comes down to it. Am I supposed to stop taking chances? Somehow, it feels like less of chance with you. I want you, Nora. Now, will you shut up and kiss me?"

I moved closer, wrapped an arm around her shoulder, and pushed my other hand into that luxuriant mass of hair. I kissed her. Kissed her without hesitancy, without little pecks on the cheek to signal my intent. I simply took her lips as if it were our hundredth kiss, rather than the second. Ger tasted of the pistachio ice cream we'd had for dessert, and her lips were mobile and soft under my own. Her tongue pushed into my mouth, urgent and seeking, and her full breasts pressed against me.

We were both panting when we broke apart. "Come home with me," she said.

We decided to walk, and the thrum of anticipation made each step a torment. We stopped to kiss in doorways, stealing a press of breast, a touch of skin. I learned what the pulse in her neck felt like under my lips, the shudder of her exhale when I touched her skin. We reached her place and took the stairs to the top floor. It was late, and we both had to work tomorrow. I had no clean clothes with me, but I didn't care. I would do the parade of pride to my desk and change into yesterday's clothes in the toilet.

Ger's flat was eclectic and comfortable. Batik and tie-dye wall hangings toned with wooden furniture and the painted walls she'd mentioned. Everything was warm, done in the tones of autumn to match her own coloring. She did have a lovely view, but I barely glanced at it. There was a narrow double bed against the window, so she could lie there and look out over London.

Ger stood by the bed and unwound the scarf from her throat, then slipped the buttons of her blouse. Her bra was the palest pink that should have clashed with her coloring, but somehow enhanced her paleness, the vividness of her hair. She reached behind and unhooked it, and it fell away to expose creamy breasts tipped with dusky pink nipples. Her skin was so pale and translucent that faint rivers of blue hazed the upper surface. She unsnapped her jeans and pulled them down, sitting on the bed to remove her boots and socks. I caught a glimpse of a bush as deeply auburn and luxuriantly curling as the hair on her head, then she stood again, proudly naked in front of me. She had the classic womanly hourglass shape, with full thighs and flaring hips. No excess weight on her stomach, which was flat and toned.

She cocked her head to one side. "Well? Are you going to stand there all night admiring the view?"

I took her in my arms, ran my hands down her curving sides, and cupped her butt. She smiled against my mouth, and her fingers pulled my shirt away from my jeans. When she bent her head back, her hair fell in curling waves and tickled my skin. I took the hint and bent to take a nipple in my mouth and sucked it to a hard point. Ger shuffled back until the bed was behind her knees and she fell backward. I lowered myself more gracefully and returned to her breasts. I circled my tongue around one nipple then moved to the other while she undid my jeans and worked her hand palm down into my knickers. The heat of it imprinted itself on my skin.

"I want you to be naked when you fuck me." There was a pause before "fuck" as if she wasn't used to saying it aloud too often. That Irish-Catholic upbringing again. I shifted enough that I could wriggle out of my jeans and underwear. It wasn't graceful, but I didn't care. I already missed the feel of her fingers on my pussy, and I rolled to lie next to her.

Ger lay on her back, one knee cocked out. The curling auburn hair between her legs was slick and wet. I brushed a finger over her pussy lips then watched her shudder. Her beautiful green eyes closed for a moment before fixing their intense gaze on my face. I pushed a finger inside her, felt the heat and moisture clasp around my finger. I added a second, then a third as she encouraged me with breathy gasps. Her hands clutched the bed cover on either side of her thighs, and she raised her hips in time with my steady thrusts. My fingers slipped easily in and out, and my thumb brushed her clit with every stroke.

I wanted it to be good for her—no, more than good. I wanted to be the best. There was already a space in my heart that belonged to her alone. This would be the first night of many I swore to myself as I watched her hips buck, her white teeth biting on her lower lip. The first night of the rest of our lives, and then I stopped thinking as Ger flew apart beneath my fingers, clenching hard around me in great wracking spasms of pleasure.

I expected her to sink down into lethargy. It was late, and such an intense climax should mean a swift descent to sleep. But she rolled over, pushed me onto my back.

"We're not done yet."

She kissed her way down my body, lingering on each nipple, pressing a line of kisses along my belly until she came to my pubes, clipped short.

"Prickly," she said and raised her face so I could see her grin and know she didn't mind.

Then she settled between my legs, and her fingers and tongue alternated their sweeps against my cunt. I was so wet there was no friction, just her tongue and its hot, wet glide, combined with the circles made by her fingers. I closed my eyes and thought of her face between my legs, of what *she* was doing to me. Of what she was doing to *me*. This was no faceless stranger giving me pleasure, this was Geraldine. My Geraldine. For that was how I already thought of her. The thoughts spun through my head, intensifying my pleasure, and my orgasm crashed over me in a minute. When its tide receded, I was sleepy, wanting nothing more than to spoon around Ger, feel her bottom pressed to my crotch, cup her full breast in my hand as we slept.

Ger maneuvered us beneath the covers, and I did spoon her. My last thoughts as I fell asleep were that the view of London from her window was indeed spectacular and that her hair smelled of vanilla.

Of course I overslept. I didn't know the best way to the office from her flat, and my haste made me clumsy. The rack of toiletries in her tiny shower went crashing to the floor when I knocked into it as I tried to soap my feet. Last night's clothes looked like charity shop rejects, and I dribbled the coffee Ger handed me down my front.

"Tonight?" I asked as I gulped coffee and tried to kiss her all at the same time. "My place?"

She nodded and pushed a piece of paper into my hand. "My mobile number. Call me."

I kissed her again, and she held my face between her hands and kissed me back deeply.

CHAPTER 6

I IGNORED THE STARES I got at work as I strutted in and grabbed yesterday's clothes from the back of my chair. After I changed, I sat at my desk, doodling on a pad while pretending to draft a court application. Ger was in my head. Her smile, her laugh, her curvy body, that luxuriant hair. In the last twenty-four hours, she'd grabbed my heart in her fist and muscled her way in. With a sigh and a goofy grin, I turned back to the application.

Sue popped her head into my office just as I finished. Although she worked in the same firm, we barely saw each other. She worked on the floor below mine, an associate solicitor with the boss from hell that made constant last-minute demands on her, usually in the booming voice that had earned him the moniker Shouting Man.

"Lunch?" she asked. "Shouting Man is in court, so he won't interrupt."

I nodded. "Give me ten minutes."

I called Ger's mobile. She answered in professional tones, "This is Geraldine." Of course, in our hasty parting this morning, I'd forgotten to give her my number. When she recognized my voice, her clipped professionalism disappeared.

"I've been thinking about you," she said, and there was warmth and honey in her voice.

"The last person who said that threatened to sue me," I joked and was rewarded by her rich chuckle.

"Good things. Very, very good things."

"Hang on to those thoughts as I hope to replace them with very, very wicked ones this evening." I'd given some thought as to where to meet her later. "There's a quiet pub about a half mile from where I live called The Moon and Sixpence. We could meet there at seven."

I gave her directions and she said she'd meet me there.

I hung up, grabbed my jacket from the back of the chair, and bounced out into the corridor to Sue. She looked sideways at me. "You look happy. You can tell me about it over a sandwich."

The day was warm and summery, one of those rare hazy days in London when the sun filters down through the buildings and the pigeons and sparrows sing in harmony. We grabbed sandwiches from the deli on the corner and went to sit by the river. The Thames flowed sluggishly past, as wide and brown as ever. Boatloads of tourists chugged by, and the commentary drifted back to us. "Here on our left is…"

Sue and I found a bench where we could talk without being overhead. She took a bite of her ham salad sandwich and chewed. "I needed that," she said. "Skipped breakfast."

"Is that skipped breakfast in a good way because you were otherwise engaged until the last moment, or skipped breakfast in a bad way because you overslept or the milk was off?"

"Bad way," she said with a grimace. "But let's talk about you first. I could do with some good news. What's made you so shiny bright this morning?"

"Remember the woman I'm going to marry?"

"I thought that was just lust. I don't think you've *ever* said the word 'marry' before unless you're talking about someone else."

"The woman I saw in the pub the other day, when you left to meet Leo. Did you make him pay, by the way?"

Sue flapped a hand. "Later. So you hit it off with this mysterious lady. Am I getting an invite to the wedding?"

"Of course. But let me ask her first."

Grated carrot flew out of Sue's mouth, to lie like confetti on my dark pants. "You're going to?"

"Yes," I said definitely. "Not yet, of course, but one day."

"You've fallen hard." Sue picked the carrot off my pants. "Sorry about the mess. So does your future wife have a name?"

"Geraldine. Ger, for short."

"She's Irish?" She shook her head. "You've landed on your feet. Not only have you fallen for someone you're in instant lust with, but it's someone your family will approve of."

"I wouldn't go that far. I don't know which part of Ireland her family is from, and there's a lot of bad blood between families floating around out there."

"You're really serious about this Geraldine, aren't you?" Sue's glance fell on my untouched sandwich. "You must be in love if you're off your tucker."

I handed her half my sandwich. "I think I am. I can't really explain it, and I don't have anything to compare it to. I've never wanted to know everything about someone before. I've never thought of spending time together past the immediate few days. And it's not just lust, before you mention it. I want to spend time with her outside of the pub or the bedroom."

Sue opened my sandwich and picked out the cucumber, flicking it away where it was swooped up by one of the ever-present pigeons. "And what does Ger think about this?"

"Way too early to say. We've only had two evenings together."

"Did you do the deed?"

"What do you think?"

"You did." Sue took a bite of my sandwich and mumbled around egg and lettuce. "That's why you're all sparkly this morning. And wearing a shirt that looks like it spent the night over your office chair."

"It did. But I don't care. I'm falling, Sue, falling in… well, something."

"Too early for it to be love." Her face settled into more somber lines and reminded me what I'd temporarily forgotten in my enthusiasm to share my happiness. "Love takes time and trust and knowledge of another person. You can't be in love, just like that. What if you found out something about her that made it impossible for you to love her? Like… I dunno, that her ex-girlfriend is a murdering psychopath wanted for the murder of three women, all of whom have shared a night with Ger?"

"Won't happen. Can't happen." I looked at Sue with as serious a look as I could muster.

She shook her head, but let it drop.

I took the opportunity to change the subject. "How are you doing?"

Truth be told, Sue didn't look so hot. Her eyes had rings of tiredness around them, and her complexion was wan as if she'd been tossing and turning all night. She flapped a hand at me. "I'm okay."

I tossed my crusts to the pigeons and swiveled to face her on the bench. "You don't look okay. You look…defeated." The word sprang into my head as I saw Sue's downcast eyes. "Tell me what the bastard's done, and I'll sic my brothers on him for you."

"He's done nothing he hadn't already spelled out for me before." When she looked up, there was a shimmer of tears in her eyes. My hard-arsed Aussie lawyer friend with tears? Things were bad.

I took her hand. "Tell me."

"When I left the pub the other night, it was because he texted he wanted to talk. Stupid gullible me thought that meant he was reconsidering. So I went around to his place with the aim of making him pay, tormenting him a little, and then reconciling in bed. Well, I tormented him, he teased me back, and somehow the serious talking never happened. We ended up fucking, of course." Sue heaved a sigh, and her eyes went distant. She took a swig from her water bottle before she continued. "And then after an hour of mind-blowing, rolling around the carpet, passionate sex, when I was ready for the cuddling up in bed part and the apologies, he told me he was happy I was seeing things his way. That he hoped we could do this again soon, but not tomorrow as he was seeing Eliza or Ellie or Eloise, some goddamned tweenie name beginning with E anyway. Then he kissed me, handed me my clothes, and said 'See ya, babe.' *Babe?*" Sue's Aussie accent tilted the word up at the end. "I'm twenty-fucking-five. I'm no one's babe. So I left. All I got out of it were two bloody awesome orgasms and carpet burns." She rested her elbows on her knees and dropped her head into her hands. "I'm not going back. Other people may be fine with that sort of relationship, but I'm not. All I'm getting is fat from eating other people's leftovers, and Shouting Man in my ear about the work I'm not doing because I can't concentrate. I missed a compliance deadline yesterday. Shouting Man had a field day with that one."

"Oh, Sue." I didn't know what to say. There was nothing I could say that would make it better. Not yet, anyway. Now was not the time to tell her she was better off without him, not while her heart leeched pain from his absence. "I'll round up the troops. Three burly London-Irish with fists like ham hocks should make him think twice about messing with you."

Sue managed a weak smile. "I'm not like you," she said. "I can't skip lightly from one person to the next. Guess I'm old fashioned like that."

I *was* like that. The thought pounded in my brain. Was. Past tense. But it had changed now that I'd met Ger.

Ger was waiting when I arrived, a bottle of shiraz and two glasses in front of her. I paused in the door and watched her at the table texting on her phone. When she saw me, she put the phone down, stood, took a pace forward, then another. We met in the middle of the room, and her arms went around my waist, mine around her shoulders, and we kissed as if we'd never part again. The kiss went on, neither of us wanting to break apart. It was only a jokey "Get a room" that penetrated the haze of lust. We broke apart, Ger's cheeks flushed and pink. The other patrons were amused, smiling, approving. There's always something heartwarming about witnessing that first flush of love.

The only place to sit was at the bar, so we had to be somewhat restrained. So instead of touches and kisses, we talked. We talked with a familiarity that betrayed our short acquaintance. It was an old sweater type of conversation as my sister Mary liked to say, where you slip into it with ease and it surrounds you with warmth.

"We have this client," I said, "who comes to see us on an almost daily basis. There's no need for that, of course, and we've tried to tell him that, while we're happy to see him, we have to

charge him. He had a fairly bad car accident, and he's convinced
he has to personally bring in every last little receipt, or to relate
in detail what went on at his last doctor's appointment. I'm now
the lucky person who has to drop everything to talk to him. He
arrived today with some receipts for expenses. When I looked
at them, I saw that among the physio and hydrotherapy receipts
there were some newsagent receipts. I looked closer—thinking
he might have bought a vehicle log book to record his travel or
something—and saw it was for porn mags. I gave them back
to him quite tactfully, saying they must have got included by
accident, but no. He wants me to claim *Playboy* and *Hustler* as
a therapy expense."

Ger sniggered. "What, he's strengthening his right wrist?"

I laughed too. "Apparently he thinks he should be allowed
to claim them as he's had to develop other interests since he can
no longer go waterskiing!"

"What did you do?"

"I said, with a perfectly straight face, that he'd have to
prove in court that he'd never had an interest in porn before
the accident, and that if the claim was large it might be
investigated. Talk to his family, for example. That's all bullshit,
of course, there's no allowance for that type of thing, even
if he'd taken up cross-stitch instead of porn. But it worked.
The thought of his mammy being asked about his newfound
pastime of masturbation was enough. He took the receipts back
and mumbled something about it being so small an expense it
probably wasn't worth claiming."

"He probably had a Tesco's bag full of receipts at home."
Ger laughed again, and I was transfixed by her wholehearted
enjoyment of the moment. How her chin tilted up when she
laughed, exposing her creamy throat.

I picked up her hand and simply held it, delighting in the way her fingers curled around mine. "What about your day?"

Her face lit up, a smile of pure delight, sourced from within. "I had a fantastic day. My boss called me into her office and said that she wanted me to come and see a new client with her, and that I would be handling the project. It's small by most people's standards—a development of three townhouses—but it's the largest project I've had control of. Obviously, she's going to be overseeing me, but I'll be running it, start to finish."

"That's fantastic."

"I'm excited—it's an amazing opportunity, but I'm a bit nervous too. What if I stuff up?"

"You won't. You obviously love your job, and it's important to you. I bet these will be the best designed townhouses in south London, and the most efficiently managed project, which will come in way under budget."

She laughed. "Oh, how I hope so." Her hand gripped mine tightly. "I'm most worried about the borough council. There's a couple of aspects of design that I'd like to include that they often seem to object to."

I listened to her talk, fascinated by her enthusiasm. While I enjoyed my work as a paralegal—notwithstanding the loopy clients—I didn't have the level of passion that Ger seemed to have about her work. Work, to me, was just a job, something that occupied me from nine to five. It wasn't my life.

Ger talked on, sketching out a couple of things on a beer mat, and I listened, trying to follow the terminology in a profession I knew nothing about.

My silence must have caught her attention. "Oh! Nora, I'm so sorry. Rabbiting on about work. You must be bored out of your skull."

"I'm not," I said honestly. "I enjoy listening to you; I love your enthusiasm. And from what you're saying, I don't think our professions are too different. You're obsessing about downpipes and door knobs, and I spent twenty minutes rewriting the same sentence in a statement yesterday. We're both focusing on the minutiae."

"The devil is in the detail."

I looked at her laughing face, her relaxed expression, the way she impatiently pushed her wild hair behind her ears, only for it to fall forward a moment later. Desire clenched in my belly, and a rampant lust surged down to my pussy. My clit throbbed—a sudden, urgent tattoo.

"Ger…"

She looked at me, and my desire for her must have been obvious, for her expression changed. Her laughter trailed away, and our gazes met, clung. Her eyes darkened, and her lips parted, as if she were forming words but couldn't say them. Words hovered on my own lips too, words it was too early to say, words that I'd never said to anyone before. A whole new layer of meaning in my life.

"I'm not hungry." Not the words sitting in the back of my throat, waiting to be said—one day.

"Me neither." She spoke softly, and her eyes never left my face.

"Come home with me."

In answer, she slid from the stool and held out her hand.

It was only a few minutes' walk to the tube station, but it took us longer. A kiss while we waited for the lights to turn green. Another, when we stopped to look at the menu in the window of a Greek restaurant. As Ger fumbled in her big bag trying to find her Oyster card, I lifted the mass of her hair and pressed a kiss to the nape of her neck. She tilted her head back, exposing the length of her neck to my lips, and another minute passed as my lips explored her skin and learned the beat of her pulse.

I wondered what she'd make of my flat, with its woeful lack of design and basic accommodations, but she didn't seem to notice. Tomás came to greet us, winding his way around our ankles in furry figure eights. While Ger made his acquaintance, I topped up his automatic food and water bowls. Then I went back to where she sat on my battered sofa, Tomás parading back and forth over her lap.

I held out my hand, and she placed hers in mine and stood. Tomás jumped down and stalked off, tail quivering, to investigate his food bowl.

"I have wine," I said, as I ran a finger from her neck to her shoulder, pushing under her T-shirt to trace the edge of her bra strap.

She shook her head and linked her hands behind my neck.

"Cheese and crackers." I bent to follow the path of my finger with my lips.

"No."

I sensed the smile on her lips. My hand came around her waist, pushing under the T-shirt, feeling skin.

"A marathon session of *The L Word* and takeaway pizza?"

"I think I'd like to see if your bedroom is as plain as the rest of your flat."

I didn't need asking twice, and I kissed her lips, dipping my tongue into her mouth to taste her sweetness. The kiss grew deep, our mouths and breath melding together, and when we broke apart the memory of the previous night flashed through my head like a widescreen movie. I wanted to see her skin again, the curve of her breasts. I wanted to push inside her, and I wanted to taste her.

I was glad I'd made an effort with housework. The room was still sparse, but at least it was tidy. Ger didn't seem to notice though. Once through the bedroom door, she came to me again, and this time when I kissed her, I undid her pants and mirrored the swoop of my tongue in her mouth with my fingers on her belly. Her hair tickled my cheek, and her hands were insistent in their own exploration, undoing my shirt, pushing it from my shoulders and then mapping patterns on my back. We moved apart long enough to shed our clothes. Ger's eyes were hot on my body as I removed my shirt, unclipped my bra and let it fall. I felt graceful under her appreciative gaze, even the normally clunky movements of shedding pants and shoes. There was no haste, and we alternated the removal of our clothes in a coordinated dance of anticipation.

Naked, we moved to the bed, lying on top of the duvet as the evening was warm. We lay facing each other and kissed again, long and slow, engaged in a tandem journey of mutual exploration. My fingers found her nipples, hers traced my slight curves, my barely-there breasts. My hands moved slowly down over her flat stomach to circle her belly button. Her fingers learned the indent of my waist and the ticklish spot just above my hip bone.

I cupped her sex, feeling her moisture against my palm, and her fingers parted my pussy lips and slid inside. We moved in the same rhythm, fingers sliding, circling, fucking, to the soft soundtrack of hums and sighs. She came before I did, her pussy fluttering around my fingers in orgasmic shivers, her breath hot on my face. And I left my fingers inside her as her fingers circled my clit and my own orgasm crashed over me.

It was still early, so after the kissing and murmurs of appreciation had faded, we rose and moved to my tiny kitchenette where I pulled out cheese, olives, and crackers and opened one of my better bottles of wine. And when the cheese was finished, we took the remainder of the wine back to bed, and the loving started again and continued into the night until the room smelled musky from our desire.

I fell asleep on my back, with Ger's hand cupping my breast and her leg thrown over mine.

CHAPTER 7

WE OVERSLEPT OF COURSE, AND any thoughts I might have had about slow and sunlit morning loving were lost in the gray light filtering in the window and Ger's panic at being late. She showered and dressed, digging clean underwear and a fresh shirt out of her big bag, while I slapped butter and Marmite on a piece of toast for her to take with her.

"My place this evening?" she said.

I nodded. It was Friday and the weekend was replete with potential for time together.

"Takeaway?" she asked. "I'm a rotten cook."

I nodded again. "But I'll cook for you on Saturday night." I hadn't even asked if she had weekend plans. Any vague plans I had were shattered and blown away so that I could spend time with Ger. She kissed me and was gone.

I drifted through my work day in a daze of anticipation. Sue was busy at lunchtime, so I worked through lunch at my desk, shoring up time so that I could leave early another day. I called Ger, but got her voicemail. She called me back when my boss was at my desk, so I didn't pick up, but her message said to come to her flat by seven that evening; she'd have the takeaway and hoped I liked Thai. I texted an affirmative and said I hoped it would include a slow cooked beef massaman. She replied it was her favorite dish, and our texts would probably have gone on all afternoon if I hadn't seen my boss's beady eyes watching me from his glass office.

I'd brought fresh clothes with me, so I didn't have to go home. I asked Sue if she fancied a drink after work, but she was heading out with a friend, so—in a definite second best—I texted my sister Mary to see if she fancied meeting. She was free, so we met in a pub halfway between her work and mine.

I was there before her and saw her enter the pub, hand in hand with a lanky, sandy-headed man. From the tight clasp of their hands, I guessed this was the famous Liam Muldoon from Kilkenny, the man who had stolen my sister's heart.

Mary said something to Liam, who turned and headed for the bar. Mary threw herself into the seat opposite me. Her eyes were shining. "I hope you don't mind, but I wanted you to meet Liam."

She radiated happiness, and when Liam returned with a bottle of a far better shiraz than I normally bought, I was immediately won over. Initially, I thought he seemed shy, almost diffident, although he scored major points from me as he was obviously as besotted with Mary as she was with him. When the bottle was nearing empty, he had loosened up enough that his wry humor came out, and it was with genuine regret I said I had to leave.

"Will you be over for breakfast on Sunday?" Mary asked. "I'm bringing Liam for the first time. It would be good if he had someone on his side from the start."

I thought of Ger and my promise to cook dinner for her Saturday night. I really didn't want to rush away on Sunday, and I didn't want to share her with my family just yet.

"Sorry," I said. "Not this week. Maybe next."

"Got your eye on someone on the far side of town?" she teased.

I gave her an enigmatic smile and left. I picked up a bottle of wine and was only a few minutes late getting to Ger's. Her flat was fragrant with Thai food and there was already a bottle of red breathing on the counter. Her small table was set for two.

She drew me inside with both hands and kissed me. My bag dropped to the floor, and I kissed her back with a swiftly escalating passion. When Ger broke the kiss, I was breathless with anticipation and happiness.

Ger moved to the counter and poured us both a glass of wine. She clinked her glass against mine. "Are you hungry? Or can I show you something special first?"

Her smile promised more than just coconut prawns and sweet chilli sauce. "Something special."

"I was hoping you'd say that. I hope you're good with heights."

"We're going to abseil down your building?"

"Not quite. Come with me, and bring your wine."

She led me to a corner of her studio, and put her glass on a shelf there. Then she grasped what looked like an ornamental wall feature of wooden bars and pulled. The whole set of bars swung away from the wall. A ladder! She flashed me a smile and started to climb. The ceiling was high, but she reached it in a few seconds. Wedging her bum against the wall, she pushed on the trapdoor. It opened and the golden light of evening spilled into the room, illuminating the dark corner. Ger climbed higher and swung herself up through the trapdoor with an ease that spoke of long practice.

"Here," she called down to me. "Put the glasses in this." A wicker basket on a rope appeared, with spaces that exactly took a wine glass. I wedged them in and she pulled the basket up smoothly. "Come on."

I set my hands to the rungs and cautiously started to climb. The makeshift ladder seemed quite sturdy. When my head came through the trapdoor, I saw Ger lounging on a blanket, her back propped against the brick chimney pot. I swung up to join her, moving slowly.

"It's safe up here, if a little illegal, so crawl, don't stand."

I didn't tell her that I had no intention of standing. We were on the roof of her studio, on a flat area about the size of a king bed, jammed between the pitch roof and the chimney. There was no railing and the edge of the roof dropped abruptly away into the nothingness. I crawled over, and she moved across enough that I could prop my back against the chimney. She handed me my wine.

"Isn't this great?"

I pressed my back against the chimney and tried not to gulp the wine. "Yeah. I think so. Or it will be once I get used to it." I'd thought the view from her top floor apartment was fantastic, but up here on the open roof was even better. London stretched away, and I could see over the roofs of the red-brick Victorian houses, over to the modern apartment blocks to the south. A river of vehicles and people moved below us, and the traffic noise seemed quieter. I groped for Ger's hand and squeezed. "How did you find this?"

"I knew the trapdoor was there when I moved in, and I guessed it was a way onto the roof, but I didn't have any way of getting up until my brother came around one day with a ladder. He also built the wall bars for me. Even the landlord doesn't know this is here—the way up just looks like decoration—I hang cloth on it when he does an inspection."

My heart rate had slowed enough that I could relax. "It's fabulous. We should have a picnic up here sometime."

The look she shot me was positively salacious. "There's lots of things we should do up here."

"As long as you don't get many helicopters going past."

"Not too many. Sometimes I come up here with a book and a glass of wine. The only time I've ever got stuck was when a gust of wind blew the trapdoor shut. I had to call my brother to rescue me. He has a key to my flat. It took him ages to come though—he was at the football and there was no way he was going to leave before the end of the game."

I thought of Brian and his fanaticism for Arsenal Football Club. "Which team?"

"Arsenal."

"My brother too. Maybe they'll go together sometime." I traced a circle on her palm with my finger. "After all, if we're together for a long, long time, they'll be friends, right?"

"Right." Her answer was a sigh, breathed into the evening air. She sounded as content as I felt, as if she too was imagining our lives together, stretching into the misty future.

I took a deep breath, waited for the familiar desire for escape to creep over me, but it was absent. It was a good feeling. For a few minutes we were silent, sipping our wine, looking out over the city, hands loosely clasped. It was as if we had known each other for a long time. There was the comfort, the familiarity of a longtime friend.

Ger finished her wine. "I don't know about you, but I'm starving."

She rose to her feet and held out a hand, pulling me up and against her body. I swayed, disorientated once again by the smallness of the space and the closeness to the edge. I held onto the chimney, while she folded up the blanket and stowed it in a tin box which she weighted down with bricks.

"After you." She gestured to the trapdoor and I was happy to oblige.

Back down in her studio, she bustled around, reheating the takeaway in the microwave. When she placed the food on the table, it included the massaman curry that I loved so much, as well as a noodle dish, and stir-fry vegetables. My mouth watered. I poured the last of the wine, and sat at her tiny, round table.

She served the food in bowls, adding her own touches of presentation—shredded kaffir lime leaves, chopped peanuts, and lime wedges.

"This looks fantastic."

"Don't be fooled. I'm a lousy cook, but I do know how to make food look good. All I can cook is stodge—a hundred ways with potatoes."

The massaman curry was melt-in-the-mouth delicious. "I'll cook you a meal," I said. "Something without a potato in sight." I forked a piece of potato from the curry and held it aloft. "Good though this is."

She wrinkled her nose. "As long as you don't cook anything with couscous."

"None," I promised. "Only things that make you crave more, that make you yearn for it, that make you beg—"

She moved around the small table and her eyes burned into mine. "Are you on the menu, Nora?"

"I could be. If you want."

"I want."

And then we were kissing again, the food forgotten, and she tasted of spice and lime and passion, and London air, distilled from a tiny rooftop space. Then of course, we were in bed together, dirty plates forgotten, and we made love against the backdrop of glass that overlooked our city.

My mobile woke me, shrill in the darkness. I groped around in the unfamiliar room until I found it, half pushed under the bed. I looked at the display, noting it was Theresa calling and it was gone midnight. The phone rang off before I could answer it, but started up again almost immediately.

"What do you want?" I grumbled into the phone. Beside me, Ger stirred and half rose on an elbow.

"Nora…" Theresa's voice was wild and desperate, even over a bad line, and there were tears in her voice. "Please come. It's Declan. He's in Emergency with a head injury."

My head spun. I wanted to ask what had happened, and would he be all right, but the tears and the desperation in Theresa's voice meant such questions would have to wait. My sister needed me. That was the important thing.

"Which hospital?"

"Charing Cross. Please, Nora, please come."

"I'll be there." I wanted to say more, but the phone had gone dead. No doubt Theresa was calling our parents, or maybe Brian. I swung my legs out of bed and started groping for my clothes.

"Nora? What's wrong?" Ger stared at me, sleepy-eyed and disheveled, her hair falling over her breasts.

"My brother's in hospital." I found my jeans and pulled them on. "That was my sister, asking me to come."

Her eyes searched my face, then she threw back the covers. "I'm coming with you."

"No," I started to say. "It will be a long night. Emergency always takes a long time—"

"Doesn't matter. If I don't come, I'll be lying here wondering if you're okay." She got out of bed and grabbed her clothes from the floor.

"I'm okay." But as I said it, I realized that I didn't have to pretend anymore. Theresa had sounded upset, and if my sister was worried, then I was worried. It was my default setting. I thought of walking into the hospital with Ger at my side, holding my hand, being there for me, and the picture was a lot more comforting than the one where I dashed in alone.

I paused dressing and held out my hand to her. She placed her hand in mine without hesitation. "Thank you. I would like it very much if you came."

We took a taxi to Charing Cross and found our way to Emergency.

"I'm here to see my brother, Declan Kelly," I said. A nurse directed us to a cubicle, where the curtains were drawn. Cold fear stole around my heart—closed curtains generally meant bad things. But then the curtain was flung back with a ferocity that could only mean one person—Theresa.

"Nora." She fell into my arms, and her tears wetted my neck. "Declan's got a head injury. It may only be concussion, but it may be a fractured skull, or even a bleed into the brain. He's had an X-ray and a CT scan and we're waiting to get the results."

I rocked her as I used to do when she was a scrappy kid with a grazed knee. "Hey, it's okay. Big sis is here now." I looked around for Ger, but I couldn't see her. "What happened?"

Theresa raised a tearstained face. "It was that fecker, Young Seánie. Who the feck else would it be? He was lying in wait for

Dec as he left the pub. Jumped him as soon as he turned the corner into Greenbridge Road. Dec didn't stand a chance. He hit the deck like a felled tree."

"Were you there?" I stroked her damp hair.

"Saw it all. Saw the punch from behind, and the second punch that felled him. Bastard. But I got him. I ran after him, and kicked him from behind. He tripped and fell into the road. There was a car coming." Theresa's voice rang with satisfaction. "The car clipped him. He's also here in Emergency somewhere."

I couldn't feel any sympathy for Young Seánie. My own family was my concern. "Have you called Mam and Da?"

"Not yet. I didn't want to worry them. If he does have a fractured skull, I'll call then."

I went into the cubicle. Dec was lying there on a hospital trolley as white as the sheets. If he'd had Charing Cross Hospital written on his face in red writing, I couldn't have picked the difference. His eyes were closed and his chest rose and fell slowly. He looked very young.

I sat next to the trolley and touched his hand. "You stupid fecker. Don't you know by now to look behind you as you enter a quiet street?"

Dec's eyes opened. "I must be in a bad way if Nora's here."

"Don't be an eejit." My eyes were damp. Allergies, I told myself, even though I knew it wasn't true. "Theresa called me."

"She's a worrier. Sorry to disappoint you, sis, but I'm going to live." His eyes closed again, and he appeared to fall asleep.

For a minute, the only sound was the beeping of the ECG machine, and someone softly crying in another part of Emergency.

Theresa sat on the chair on the other side of Dec's trolley. "If you get better, I'm going to kill you." She directed her words to Dec, but apart from a twitch of his lips, he didn't reply.

A nurse swept aside the curtains, and a doctor in a white coat entered. He scarcely looked as old as Dec, and his chin was covered in bum fluff. He had a chart in his hand, and he smiled down at Dec. "I've got good news for you. You must have a very thick head. There's no fracture, no bleeding on the brain. You're a very lucky man—it looks as if you've escaped with concussion. We're going to keep you here until morning, and then all being well, you can go home."

Dec managed a weak smile. "Thanks, Doc."

"So no need to dig the hole yet?" I directed my question to the doctor, but it was the nurse who answered. "Not unless his sister here wants to bury him alive for scaring her."

Theresa had the grace to look ashamed. "Not this week." She hesitated. "Nora, now we know Dec's okay, if you wouldn't mind staying here for a minute, I'm going to see if I can find out what happened to Young Seánie."

"Your friend who was clipped by the car?" None of us corrected her assumption about being friends. "He's okay. Nothing serious. His sister is here too." The nurse left the cubicle.

Theresa met my eyes, and her earlier bravado was gone. "I'll stay here then," she muttered. "I don't want to meet any of the Flannerys. You go home, Nora. I probably interrupted... well, something."

"Girl sex," I said with a straight face, even though it wasn't technically true. I'd been asleep when Theresa's call came.

Theresa's slight smile was worth the lie. "Yeah, get back to your girl sex—if she'll let you back in the door."

CHAPTER 8

I WONDERED WHERE GER WAS. She'd been with me as we entered Emergency. I guessed she hadn't wanted to intrude on a private family moment, or maybe the nurse had limited the number of visitors. I figured she was out in the main waiting area. For a second I thought about introducing Ger to the twins, but it wasn't really the time or the place. I stood and hugged Theresa and kissed Declan on the cheek. "Want me to call Mam and Da?"

"No." Declan was definite. "No point worrying them. I'll be out of here tomorrow, before they even notice I'm missing."

I waggled fingers at both of them in farewell and went back to the main waiting area. There was no sign of Ger. I figured she'd gone to the loo or something, but she appeared a minute or so later. She looked pale and subdued, but I figured it was due to the harsh hospital lighting and the lateness of the hour.

"Sorry I wasn't here."

I took her hand and pulled her close for a hug. She was stiff at first, which I put down to the hospital setting, but then she softened in my embrace, and her arms raised to hold me tight, so very tight. We rocked together for a minute, and then I eased away.

"Declan is going to be okay," I said. "No major head injury, nothing broken."

She nodded, and we left the hospital. There was a taxi rank outside, so we slid into the first one, and Ger gave her address.

"What happened?" she asked.

"He was punched from behind. Not a random attack. My family has been feuding with another Irish family for three generations. My grandfather came over from Ireland with his friend, and they worked on the same building site. But they fell out when his friend was promoted to foreman and then sacked my grandfather. Our families have hated each other ever since."

Geraldine had gone still, her gaze on my face.

"The Flannerys don't live too far from my parents' house. As kids, we went to the same school of course, and there were playground fights most days. Now, not so much, but every so often, something erupts, and it's usually between Declan and one of the Flannery boys."

"Do you buy into the feud?"

I shrugged. "No. I think they should let things pass. I only know a couple of the kids by sight now, so how can I feud with them? But my parents are deadly serious about it. My mam told me when I was fourteen that I could date whomever I wanted—girl, boy, someone in between, just as long as they weren't a Flannery. My parents still mean that. To them, the feud is as alive as it ever was."

"So do you care what happened to the Flannery boy?" asked Ger.

It was a strange question, but I answered anyway. "Theresa asked—I think she felt guilty, as she pushed him into the road and he got hit by a car—but the nurse said he's okay. Which is good. He's a mean bugger, by all accounts, but I still wouldn't want anything too bad to happen to him."

"A feud." Ger stared straight ahead, to where the lights of London traffic weaved through streets that never really slept.

"Yeah. I know how medieval it sounds, but you don't know my family." The taxi swerved around a red London bus, throwing Ger against me. I wrapped an arm around her, buried my face in her hair. "I'm so glad I found you," I mumbled.

The smallest of sighs, and then her hand fumbled for mine, squeezed and released. The taxi drew to a halt outside her flat. There was the barest streak of dawn in the sky—the night had rolled over to morning while we were in the hospital. My stomach rumbled. "Fancy getting breakfast?" I asked. "There's a place I know near here that opens early for the nightclub crowd. They do a great bacon and egg roll—you need a wheelbarrow to get it home."

She shook her head. "Maybe later. Let's go up. I'm a bit tired."

We took the stairs in silence, but once in the hallway outside her flat, Ger's lethargy seemed to lift. She was all over me; her hands ran over my backside and pressed between my legs as she kissed me, her lips hard on mine. I took the key from her hand and tried to fit in the lock. If we didn't get inside soon, we might give the neighbors a show they wouldn't forget in a hurry. The door swung open finally, and we stumbled inside. Her hands stripped me of my jacket, pulled my shirt out of my pants, undid the buttons, and tugged it off my shoulders. Her mouth latched onto mine and stifled anything I might have said. But there was nothing to say. The heat rose in my blood and my passion exploded to match hers. There was urgency and desire in her actions, kisses hot and heated, and a strange sort of desperation leaking from her. As if there wasn't much time.

"Slow down," I tried to say, but she stopped my words with a kiss and pulled my pants open so fiercely the button shot across the floor.

She dragged me over to the bed by my open pants and yanked them down. In a flurry of movement, she pushed me onto my back on the bed, fell on top of me, and buried three fingers in my cunt.

"Come for me, Nora. Come for me." Her words had the tone of an order. Her fingers pistoned, and she settled her mouth on my breast and bit hard, leaving a rosy purple mark on my skin.

"My darling, come for me." There was a choke in her voice, but my orgasm was building inexorably, a hard edge of lust, a sweet shaft of desire. Her urgency infected me, and in only a couple of minutes, I was flying into white heat under her fingers.

She left her fingers inside me and shuffled until she could put her mouth to my pussy, gentling me through the aftershocks with slow sweeps of her tongue. The intensity was mind blowing.

When I could breathe again, I encouraged her up to lie by my side, and kissed her slowly. Our lovemaking thus far had been frantic, swift, and urgent. I wanted to slow it down. I kissed her languorously, moving my lips slowly, trailing my fingers under the collar of her blouse, a gentle seduction. Each button that I undid meant another kiss on exposed skin.

Ger shivered and shifted restlessly underneath me, but let me set the pace. I wondered if fast and hot was her preferred pace of lovemaking. When her breasts were exposed, I spent a long time kissing each pink tip, curling my tongue around the nipple, sucking in their sweetness, and running my fingers around her voluptuous curves.

By the time I worked my way down between her legs, she was flushed and panting. She was sodden, her knickers damp, her bush moist. I lapped her juices like a cat, and as she had done, used fingers and tongue to bring her to her peak. But where Ger had been fast and direct, I took the long and winding road. I kissed her inner thighs, fluttered my fingertips over her mound, and trailed them along her engorged pussy lips. Only when she started begging did I push my fingers inside her and sucked her clit into my mouth. When she came, I placed one hand on her belly in a vain attempt to keep her still. I rode her bucking hips, and her cries were sweet in my ear.

Afterwards, I was starving hungry although Ger didn't seem focused on food. Her flat was cool, so I pulled my shirt back on which gave me some warmth. Ger dressed again.

"Breakfast." I found eggs in her fridge and a half loaf of bread, and set about scrambling the eggs with some dried herbs I found in the cupboard, and made instant coffee.

Ger seemed subdued, but I put it down to tiredness. We ate breakfast sitting at the counter.

When the food was gone, Ger slid off the stool. "It's time for you to go."

My surprise must have been evident. "I thought we'd do something together today. Do you already have plans?"

"It's not that." She wouldn't meet my eyes. "It ends here."

I stared at her in puzzlement. "What are you talking about?"

"Us. You and me. This ends here, today."

Something cold moved through my chest, and the coffee and food roiled in my stomach. "What do you mean? What was all that talk about how lucky we are to find each other? Was that crap, then?"

My stomach churned hard, and I thought I might throw up.

"Not crap, no. But this can't continue."

I stared at her, the shock of her words making my reply harsh. "You've just changed your mind? Is this how you get your kicks? Was all that talk about being worried I'd break your heart just a way of suckering me in? You must have laughed inside when I said you were special. I'm falling for you, Ger. Love. Not lust. *Love*."

She looked at me then, and her eyes were moist and swimming. She wiped her eyes with a jerky movement. "Do I look like I'm laughing? Do I?"

Her voice was torn and ragged, and despite the ringing in my ears and the taste of horror on my tongue, I saw her misery. My defensive anger subsided, and I took her hand. "Then what? Do you have a girlfriend already?"

That I could battle. That I would win.

The tears overflowed, and she wiped her eyes on her free sleeve. An endearing, childlike gesture that had a faint familiarity to it. I frowned.

Ger wrenched her hand free as if what she had to say was best done without touching me.

"Nora Kelly." She clutched the edges of her shirt, as if it might split. Like my heart. "Nora *Kelly* meet Geraldine *Flannery*. My brother is Young Seánie." She stood, and I saw the shake in her fingers, even as they clutched her shirt. "If it's any consolation, I didn't recognize you either. We would have been eleven the last time we had much to do with each other, and we both look very different now."

She was a Flannery. The weight of inevitability settled like gravel in my gut. Of all the women in the borough, in London, in the world, my soul mate turned out to be my family's sworn enemy. I swallowed hard around the boulder in my throat. I remembered Geraldine Flannery. She was in my class at primary school, a skinny kid with big eyes and ginger plaits. We would hurl insults at each other from opposite ends of the playground, while our stick-limbed and scabby-kneed brothers fought in the middle, tearing into each other until the teacher pulled them apart. I remembered dinnertimes at home, my Da asking my brothers how many Flannery boys they'd bested that day. I was sure it had been the same in Ger's house.

I'd hardly seen her since we were eleven. We'd gone to different secondary schools. I had been sent to the convent to be tortured by nuns, and I assume Ger had been sent to the other Catholic school, a short distance away. I'd only seen her in passing since then, and not at all for a good few years. Different universities, growing up, moving out had seen to that.

"When did you realize?" My voice was thick with misery.

"At the hospital. You asked for Declan *Kelly*. I wondered if you were one of *those* Kellys, but figured it must be a coincidence—it's not an uncommon name, after all. When you went off to see Declan, the nurse stopped me, saying he was only allowed two visitors. I went back to the waiting room, and as I did, I heard Young Seánie's voice. I went to see him. He told me what happened—yes, even the part when he went for Declan from behind. Young Seánie's got a broken wrist, caused by your sister pushing him under a car. He'll be okay—no thanks to Theresa. Once I knew he was going to be okay, I went back to the waiting room."

All I could think was that the woman I was falling for, the woman I knew I was destined to be with, was dumping me. We could have surmounted so much, but not this. Never this. But even though I thought it was hopeless, I had to try.

"That's our families. Not us. We're different. We *mean* something to each other, not just someone to torment, someone to fight. You and me, together. Can you look me in the eye and tell me the last few days have meant nothing to you?"

"No, I can't. You must know that. But equally, this can't go on."

"We can do this. It doesn't have to be the end. This stupid feud between our families…it's time it ended. It was our grandparents, for feck's sake. Not you, not me."

She nodded. "You're right. But you told me your parents would rather see you dead than date a Flannery. If we keep seeing each other—"

"Marry," I interjected. "If we marry. This isn't just sex and a good time."

"That makes it worse." Her eyes were red rimmed and tears fell unchecked down her cheeks. "If it were just a fling we could have that and move on. But it's not. I'm falling in love with you, Nora, and you know what that means—family dinners, big Irish gatherings. Can you imagine our parents together in one room without killing each other? Our brothers? We might get past this, you and me, but our families? They'd sooner see the pope hanged as a heretic."

"Then it will be just you and me. We don't have to tell them."

She shook her head; even her red curls were subdued. "No. I won't be ashamed of the woman I love. If we were together, we'd be saying goodbye to our families forever. I can't do that. My family is everything to me. I can't imagine not having them in my life."

My stomach roiled again, and the scrambled eggs threatened to make a reappearance. There was an insistent refrain in my head—don't let her end it; don't let her end it. "At some point in everyone's life, family takes second place to a partner."

"But family is still there for most people. I always expected that any partner of mine would love my family as I do, and be a part of my family. And I looked forward to being a part of theirs." Her eyes fixed on the dirty breakfast plates on the counter. "You're asking me to amputate a major part of myself."

"I'll do it for you." The taste of desperation filled my dry mouth. "I'll be a part of your family. I'll love them as I do my own."

She was already shaking her head. "You're a *Kelly*. They won't give you the time of day. And I couldn't ask you to cut yourself off from your family when I'm not prepared to do it. Even if we somehow got past that, every time we saw Declan, or Theresa, or Young Seánie we'd remember. Your sister broke my brother's wrist. My brother gave your brother a serious head injury. How can we not be involved? Do you think we'd have cozy family gatherings, our brothers lifting pints together and going to the football? It would be mayhem. It would be hate and anger and eventually, even if we tried to keep out of it, you and I would be sucked in."

"We could keep them apart. See them separately."

"Keep a score chart of who'd invited who where? What about important family things—Christmases, birthdays. Anniversaries? Young Seánie and Declan will come to blows again—that's as sure as death and taxes. What if next time, it's not just a broken wrist and a minor head injury? What if next time one of them is seriously hurt? Would you be able to live with me if, say, my brother put yours in a wheelchair? Because I'm not sure I could live with you if the reverse happened."

"Ger, please, I..."

Her mouth twisted. "To think I was worried that you would break my heart. You're not, Nora. I'm breaking my own."

I felt dampness on my cheeks and realized I must be crying. Me, tough Nora, who remained dry-eyed at funerals and weepy movies alike. "You're breaking mine too. Please, Ger, there must be something we can do, some—"

"I'm sorry, but I can't." She took a pace forward, reached up, and brushed her mouth over mine. "I'm sorry, Nora."

There was nothing left to say. I went over to the bed and dressed, found my phone, picked up my bag, and returned to where Ger still stood. She was facing the window, her arms wrapped tightly around her middle. She didn't look around.

I turned and left, and the soft closing of the front door had more finality than if she had slammed it behind me.

CHAPTER 9

I THREW MYSELF INTO MY work during the weeks that followed. I went in early, stayed late, and drank less as a result. My boss approved and made noises about increasing my file load and giving me a pay rise. I made the appropriate expression of appreciation, but I didn't care. Work was just a way of filling the day, stuffing my mind with things that didn't matter until it was time to go home to bed.

Sue appeared at my office door one evening. It was gone six, and everyone else had left for the day. With a guilty start, I realized I'd barely seen her since Ger left me. We'd had lunch a couple of times and talked mainly about how she was doing. But as soon as she'd asked me about Ger, it was too much. I'd given her the bare facts of the feud and the situation, and then I'd changed the subject. Sue had nodded and not pushed.

"Get your jacket, Kelly, we're off of the pub. You and me. All these long hours aren't right. You're making the rest of us look bad."

I took one look at her face, saw her concern for me overlying her own still raw sadness, and acquiesced. I saved the file note I was writing midsentence and shut down my computer. Sue and I walked through the office, past the darkened computers, teetering piles of briefs, and overflowing files. We went to a pub around the corner, and Sue ordered a bottle of cabernet and two bags of salt and vinegar crisps.

"*Sláinte*," she said, mangling the pronunciation of the Irish word. "To us and the mess we're making of our lives."

"Cheers," I said in return.

The wine was robust, a rich red, better than our usual bottle of plonk, and the crisps were welcome. My stomach was telling me I'd skipped lunch.

Sue waited until I'd relaxed into my seat. "Tell me."

The raw pain of Ger's absence pushed its way into my throat. "You first."

She managed a weak smile that was a feeble echo of her usual spontaneous grin. "You are looking at Sue Brent, newly and officially single, who hasn't had sex since Leo called me 'babe,' which was three weeks, one day and," she checked her watch, "about twenty-one hours ago. On the plus side, Shouting Man should be renamed Louder Than Normal Man, and he even gave me a compliment the other day on my handling of the witnesses in the Deger case."

I clinked glasses with her. "And the minus side?"

Her face crumpled. "I still miss the bastard. My head knows it wasn't working; my heart wants him back. I bumped into him the other morning at the tube station. He was with someone, kissing her goodbye on the platform. They'd obviously spent the night together. The bastard introduced her to me."

"Was it the same woman as before? Ellie or Elspeth or whatever her name was?"

"No. It was a different name." Sue sighed out a long shuddering breath that stirred the empty crisp packets. "And that's my answer, so you don't need to point it out. He's no intention of settling down with anyone. He's playing the field, big time."

I thought of Leo, whom I'd met a few times. Charming, in a distracted way, and good looking if you liked the blond and boyish sort. But even then his eyes had flitted around the room. I recognized the type; after all, it was the way I used to operate BG—Before Ger.

"You need to move on." I folded the crisp packet into a pleat and let it spring back. "But it's easier said than done."

"Maybe I should fall for a woman next time."

"You think we have it easier?" The rock was back in my throat again. "Think female drama times two."

"You always seemed to float above it though. I envied you."

Past tense. "I wasn't involved. I was the Leo in relationships. Flitting around, meeting and greeting, bedding not wedding."

"But not anymore." Sue's words weren't a question.

"Not any more. Why does it hurt so fecking much?"

Sue sipped her wine. "Because you care, because I do. But I'm sick of it. Sick of getting my heart broken. Why do I always fall for the ones who are just after a good time? Just for once I'd like someone to care more for me than I do for them."

"I should introduce you to my brother, Brian," I said. "He's always falling for the wrong ones as well."

"I know how he feels."

I studied Sue, her blunt, honest face, her short cropped hair and tomboy look. When I'd first met her, I'd thought she was into women, but Sue was straight. Or so she said. She had no problem with lesbians; she sometimes came to dyke bars with me to play pool, and she got on fine with my friends. If a woman hit on her—which happened quite often—she'd smile and shrug and say "Sorry, I'm straight."

"Would you date a woman?" I asked.

She hooted. "You just warned me away."

"But would you?"

It was her turn to fiddle with the crisp packet as if the hard questions could only be answered with the veneer of distraction.

"I have a hard enough time with romance without adding another variable into the mix."

I dropped the subject and, for a minute or two we were both silent, sipping our wine and contemplating our failed love lives. Or at least I was.

Sue propped her chin on her hand. "So what are you going to do about Ger?"

"I don't know." I sighed. "The choices are go back to my wild and winning ways and forget about her or keep working myself into an early grave, get rich, and retire to the Bahamas where the women are doubtlessly gorgeous and don't have a single Irish gene in their bodies."

"I wouldn't be too sure about that," said Sue. "Wasn't there some shipwreck of Irish convicts on their way to Australia?"

"If so, they must have been a long way off course. I hope they sacked the navigator."

"Why aren't you talking about the third option?" Sue leaned forward, nearly knocking over the wine. "Fight for her. Get her back. You keep saying she's the love of your life, but you threw in the towel at the first hurdle."

"I can't fight family. And that's what I'd be up against. Mine and hers—I'd be disowned. So would she."

Sue drummed her fingers on the table. "In this day and age? Really? They didn't throw you out of the house when you came out to them, and that's surely a greater issue in their eyes."

"True," I admitted. "But it wasn't easy, and there were a lot of prayers said for my soul. But they came around."

"Surely that has to be harder than dating a Flannery?"

"You'd think so. But our families are like fox terriers. They don't give up when they sink their teeth in, and they're good at hate. I tried, Sue, I really tried. Ger shot down every argument I made."

After that, there seemed little to say on the matter, and by unspoken consent, Sue and I changed the subject and spent the rest of the bottle of wine bitching about work. But her words resonated in my head. Was I giving up too easily? I was twenty-eight. I was born in London, and while Ireland was my heritage, a place I loved to visit, I wasn't truly a part of it. I wasn't bound by the restrictions my family had brought with them.

But the next day, in the gray London morning made grayer by a crashing hangover from the second bottle of red we'd drunk, it didn't seem so easy. As I walked to the station, I was determined to move on. Forget Geraldine, forget her red hair, her laugh, her curvy body. Forget all that we had in common. And most of all, I'd shift her from my heart where she had lodged herself. I'd never had any problem forgetting women in the past—I'd just go out and have a good time and find another woman for however long it lasted. Love? I wasn't in love with Geraldine—I couldn't be. We'd only had four dates. That was nowhere near long enough to be in love, to build a relationship, to plan a life together, despite what I'd believed at the time.

I pushed down the tiny voice hammering at my heart that said yes, it was long enough, and that Ger was different. I ignored the ache in my chest that missed her presence. I tamped down the surge of hope whenever I saw a flame of hair in a crowd.

And I went out to pick up a woman.

CHAPTER 10

I HADN'T BEEN BACK TO my old haunt in weeks. Not since BG. The dyke bar I frequented had the same crowd of lesbians hanging out, playing pool, eyeing each other up, and rating any newcomers who came in. London was a big revolving door, and there was always someone new. I went alone because I always found people I knew there, and this time wasn't an exception. The first person I saw as I entered was Tash, my ex-friend-with-benefits who had stopped returning my calls. She shot me a frosty glance and turned her back, and her voice grew more animated as she chatted to friends. Although I didn't think I'd strung her along—I'd always been upfront and honest about how I perceived our relationship—I had a twinge of guilt at how I'd obviously hurt her.

I joined a gang of mates at the pool table and put my name on the challenge board. There was a girl there who played pool as if she were born to it. American, judging by her accent and her laughing comments about the difference between American and Brit rules. Small, with big hair and a wide grin, she was obviously having a great time, holding the table by winning time and time again. We played for drinks, and her bourbon and cokes marched in an orderly row around a side table, appearing faster than she drank them. I sipped my wine while

I waited my turn and watched her. She appeared to be alone, a tourist maybe. Perfect. Although judging by the interest, I wasn't the only one who thought so.

When it was my turn, she said hello and stuck out a hand. It was small and cool, and her smile was wide.

"Monica," she said. "Most people call me Moni." She chalked her cue. "Let's see what you've got."

Her flirting was automatic, and although her eyes flicked up and down my body, I could see she was enjoying the evening and wasn't making any definite attempt to hook up.

"Nora," I said in reply, and held her hand a moment longer than necessary.

From what I'd seen of her play, she was good. But I'm a pretty decent pool player, and I thought I had a fair chance of winning.

I chalked my cue and, as the challenger, lined up for the break. Two yellow balls spun into corner pockets.

Moni raised an eyebrow. "Not the first time you've played then."

I didn't answer; instead I concentrated on lining up the next shot into the center pocket. I felt her eyes on my backside as I bent over the table to pocket the yellow ball cleanly. I had a choice on the next shot—easy into the top pocket or a tricky spin into a middle pocket. Remembering her intense gaze as I'd stretched for the last shot, I opted for the spin. It meant I had to reach over the table, enough that my shirt pulled out of my jeans, exposing a line of skin. I lined up. I missed.

Moni strolled around the table sizing up her shot. "Nice try," she said before she picked off two reds in quick succession.

A red ball came to rest alongside the cushion, nuzzled up to one of my yellows.

Moni shot me an audacious glance from under lowered lashes. "In bed together already."

I smiled in response, a lazy grin accompanied by a slow hooding of my eyes; an expression that often worked for me. It seemed to have the desired effect as there was an extra jut of her backside as she hooked a leg up on the table to reach for the shot. And missed.

I took a sip of my wine, the familiar exaltation of the chase coursing through my blood. *She's mine*, I thought, and waited for the thrum of lust to start its tattoo of desire in my belly. But there was nothing. I took a larger gulp of wine and let my eyes roam Moni's body in blatant invitation. Usually at this stage, the throb of my clit and pulse of need would make me force a quick end to the game and lead my opponent to a quiet table at the rear to get better acquainted. An acquaintance of the kissing and touching kind. But I felt nothing, except a kind of sadness, a gray mist of loneliness, despite the crowded bar.

I pushed the feeling aside and took my shot without taking care to line it up correctly. And missed.

"Impatient," she said, with a thread of laughter in her voice.

I dragged a deep breath, and forced down an image of bright auburn hair and superimposed it with a wild blond mane. "Maybe," I said.

Moni chalked her cue and then, from the other side of the table, pressed the tip to my forehead. "Oops," she said. "I seem to have marked you as mine."

She was all business as she efficiently sank the remaining reds and lined up for the black. "Bank shot, center pocket."

"You don't have to call your shots in Britain."

"I know, but old habits die hard." She executed a neat bank shot, and the black ball spun into the pocket.

She straightened, and I held out a hand. "Good game. I'll get your drink. Bourbon and coke?"

Moni gestured to the parade of glasses on the table. "I think I've got enough here for two. Why don't you help me drink them while I tell you about some of my other old habits?"

The invitation was obvious. BG my response would have been a slow smile and a drawled "Now that's my sort of invitation," and I would have wrapped an arm around her shoulders, and we would have retreated to one of the booths at the back of the pub, which was a signal that you wanted to be left alone.

But I didn't want to. The thought of flirtatious conversation, kisses, a feel of thigh, a squeeze of breast, touches and tastes and caresses with the conclusion already known, held little appeal. But I was here to get over Ger and getting back out there was an important step. Replacing her in my bed was the first step to replacing her in my life, and eventually, I hoped, she would fade from my heart.

I nodded and scooped up three of the drinks.

Moni turned to the girl hovering for the next game. "Sorry," she said, "I'm collecting my winnings and going. The table's all yours."

We grabbed a corner booth, and Moni slid onto the bench next to me instead of sitting opposite. Her thigh pressed against mine, and her hand rested familiarly on my jeans. A finger ran the length of the inseam. "Now we can get to know each other better."

It was a strange feeling to be on the receiving end of such intense flirtation. Usually I was the one leading, pushing, enticing, all with the aim of a highly satisfactory end to the evening. Moni was a pro, and she was obviously as sexually dominant as I was. I pushed aside the thought of a curvy body and milk white skin, of the give and take that had characterized our brief time together. I focused on Moni. Ger was my past. Moni, and women like her, were my future.

"There's nothing much to know." I picked her hand from my inner thigh and turned it over to press my lips to her palm. My tongue flickered out to taste. "I'm a Londoner, I live and work here. You, however..."

"Dallas, Texas," she said. "If this were a dyke bar over there, I'd be wearing cowboy boots and a hat, and my hair would be even bigger. I'm on a two-week tour of Europe, and I have two nights in London. This is the first." She gave me a heated look from under her eyelashes. "So you know exactly what you're getting."

Perfect. A stranger to ease me back into the wild world of casual sex that left my heart safely alone.

I turned to face her on the bench seat, and in that moment, a picture flashed in my head of Ger and how she'd made the same move on our second date. I swallowed and pushed Ger out of my head. I leaned forward and pushed my hands into Moni's hair, winding the fine strands around my fingers, and anchoring her head. My lips hovered close, ready to kiss her.

"I know exactly what I'm getting," I whispered against her lips. "And I like it a lot."

She kissed me hard then, taking no prisoners. Her lips pushed against mine until I opened my mouth and let her in. Moni was all heat and determination, all fierceness and passion. She knew what she wanted, and she was out to get it. The kiss went on in a clash of teeth and exchange of saliva, wet and hot. I gave it my all, trying to slow the kiss down, trying to sink into it and lose myself in the sex haze that normally started its slow burn about now. But there was nothing.

I released her hair, and Moni pulled back. She settled back against the bench and picked up a bourbon and coke. I did the same. The ice was melting fast, but I swirled it around the glass and skulled the drink. The heat of the bourbon warmed my stomach.

"You're some kisser." Moni drank hers at a more decorous pace than me. "I can't wait to see how you use your lips in other ways."

"And you have to show me your other bad habits."

She leaned forward and put her lips to my ear. "Don't let my looks deceive you. I'm a top, and my strap-on is in my suitcase at the hotel."

The first frisson of desire trickled down between my legs at her words. I couldn't remember the last time anyone had fucked me like that. Usually I was the one on top, harness in place. But even that was rare. For the most part, I preferred to use fingers and tongue, a hand or fist, skin on skin, rather than toys and strap-ons. But they had their place, and right now, the thought of being fucked by a petite femme seemed…appealing.

Maybe having someone else take control was what I needed.

I picked up another bourbon and, without releasing the lock of our eyes, drank it down. "I think you need to drink up, Miss Moni from Texas, and then let's figure out how we get to your hotel."

I'd expected her to be staying in one of the suburban budget hotels with a room the size of a wardrobe and a shared bathroom, but she hailed a taxi and gave directions to one of the larger chains just off the West End. Obviously, she had money as a night here would be most of my week's entertainment budget. Her room on the twelfth floor had a queen bed with a window that overlooked London. The view was different, but I was taken back to the nights I'd spent in Ger's flat, surrounded by her good taste and beautiful things, and the view of the lights of London.

I turned from the window to see Moni advancing with a bottle of wine, and two tumblers.

"I love this view," she said. "Dallas is a big city, but it doesn't have the soul that London does. Every time I turn a corner here, I'm walking into another bit of history." She handed me one of the tumblers and splashed some wine into both of them. "And so many women. I should move here."

She seemed more natural when she wasn't flirting. "Have you lived anywhere other than Dallas?" I asked her.

"College in Portland. That's it. Until now. I'm maxing my college loans with this trip. Seeing a little bit more of the world."

We moved to the bed and propped ourselves against the headboard. The edge of lust that had encircled Moni in the bar seemed doused. Now she was just a pretty woman with a lovely accent and, it turned out, a wicked sense of humor. She regaled me with tales of college escapades, and I retaliated with the tale of when Sue and I had bluffed our way into the royal enclosure at Ascot, and Sue, the anti-royalist Aussie she was, had told Princess Anne that the monarchy was as much use as tits on a bull. We'd been thrown out about two seconds after that, but Princess Anne's astonished face remained etched in our memories.

Before I knew it, the bottle was empty. Moni blinked. "When did that happen?"

"Where's your strap-on?" I asked at the same time, and we both howled with the sort of lunatic hilarity that drunkenness brings.

Moni snuggled up to me. "I lied. I don't have one. Imagine if they'd pulled it from my bags at Heathrow."

I wrapped an arm around her shoulders, pulled her close, kissed the top of her head, and we were both silent. It was a shared, companionable silence. I was starting to doze off against the headboard, so I slid down the bed, taking her with me.

"We should…that is, we came back here to fuck," Moni said, the words muffled by my breast as she snuggled in closer and wrapped herself around me. "But I'm too tired."

"Me too." I tried to reconstruct the first frisson of lust I'd felt as we left the pub, but it had evaporated like frost on a May morning. I didn't want sex, I realized. This unlikely companionship from a stranger felt good. It felt like a friend. It could have been Sue here with me, asleep on my shoulder and muttering nonsense into my chest.

The wine on top of the bourbon was having an effect and making it hard to move. With an effort, I pushed Moni away long enough to wriggle out of my shoes, socks, and jeans, and remove my bra from under my T-shirt. I contemplated Moni. She was asleep, snoring softly, her blond hair spread over the pillow. I picked one long strand of it off my T-shirt and bent to remove her footwear and jeans. I didn't attempt her bra, just left her in T-shirt and knickers. With a lot of tugging, I managed to get the duvet out from underneath her and spread it over the top of us.

CHAPTER 11

I was disoriented in the morning. Light filtered in the window, a muted gray London morning. My mouth felt like the bottom of a birdcage, and there was a weight on my chest. It was Moni, laying half across me, still sound asleep. For a moment I couldn't remember where I was or what we had done last night. Did we have sex? The night was all too hazy. But as the light spread through the window, and my memory became clearer; I recollected the unexpected easy companionship we'd shared.

I should be disappointed. Here was a sweet and hot babe in my bed, and all we'd done was talk, get drunk, and fall asleep. But there was another feeling—relief that I hadn't cheated on Ger. Cheated. I snorted quietly so as not to wake my companion. It wasn't cheating if the other party had already broken up with you and, indeed, wanted nothing more to do with you. It was moving on. But, I realized, I wasn't ready for that. Not yet. I still had Ger in my heart, and as long as she was lodged there, my body was hers.

I started to move, edging my way out from underneath Moni. When I made it to the edge of the bed, she was still asleep. I padded around the room, finding a kettle and instant coffee in a cupboard. Moni woke as I poured boiling water into two cups.

"Morning, lover," she sang. Then her smile twisted in puzzlement. "Or morning, not-lover." Her hands did their own explorations over her body, checking out her clothing.

"Milk and sugar?" I asked.

"Just cream. Milk. Whatever."

I put UHT milk into both cups and came back to the bed.

"That was some night," she said, as she made room for me against the headboard. "Lots to drink, good conversation, hot sex with a beautiful woman."

"Two out of three ain't bad, right?"

"Yeah." She sipped her coffee. "I'm sorry about last night. It was obvious why you came back to my room, and I bailed on you. It's not that I didn't want to... Aw, heck, I did want to get down and dirty with you... It's just that..." She pinched the bridge of her nose. "I'm making a mess of this."

"It's okay. I think my fumbling explanation would be similar to yours. I have a hell of a headache, but my memory of the evening goes like this—we flirted, we kissed, we came back to your room. We talked, we drank more. We talked more. We drank even more. Then we fell asleep."

"That's about it. I feel I owe you an explanation. There was a bit of omission in my story last night. I am from Dallas, and I am over here on a two-week tour of Europe, but what I didn't say was it's in an attempt to get over my ex who dumped me rather abruptly." Moni closed her eyes and leaned her head back against the headboard. "She took up with my brother." Her eyes opened, blue, piercing, and rather beautiful despite being so bloodshot. "My fucking brother! Talk about keeping it in the family. I couldn't stand to think about it, let alone see them together, so I acted like I didn't care and booked a trip to Europe. I was determined to find a woman, or several, have some nights to remember over here to wash her out of my head." She sighed and whispered in a small voice, "as you can see, it's not working too well."

My newly fragile heart bled a little for her, and I wanted to take her in my arms and hold her. Not for any other reason than to comfort her. "Did you know your ex was bisexual?"

"Oh yeah. I was her first woman. She'd only been with men before me. Never again. I'm never going to fall for anyone ever again who isn't a rainbow-wearing, pink-triangle-tattooed dyke on a bike who can show me her HRC card and whose relationship resumé is entirely full of XX chromosomes. Someone, I suspect, exactly like you."

"I don't have a bike license, and I'm not sure what the HRC is, but I can guess."

"Big queer rights organization in the States. I'm sorry, Nora, I was using you, trying to get over Em, but when it came down to the big dirty part of the night, I just couldn't. You're the most attractive woman I've seen in a long time. I love how you look, how you dress, your cute Brit accent, your wide shoulders. God, you're gorgeous—exactly my type. And you must be horny and frustrated as hell after I effectively bailed on you."

I couldn't help it; I started to laugh, my shoulders shaking in silent mirth. I could sense Moni's eyes on me in affronted bewilderment. She'd just confessed she was pining for her ex, and I was laughing.

"Sorry," I said. "We're a pair of eejits, both of us. It's just that your story sounds so like mine. I should be apologizing to you."

Her hurt demeanor eased. "Tell me."

"My girlfriend left me too. I was falling for her hard, and I think she was falling just as hard for me. She didn't leave me for anyone else; she left because I'm a Kelly and she's a Flannery and our fecking stupid Irish families have been feuding for fecking *ever* with no end in sight. Our families would disown us if we dated. I would take that chance, but Ger won't. So she left." It was my turn to sigh into my cooling coffee. "I was in the pub last night for the same reason as you—trying to pick up a woman to help me forget. And you're just my type, Moni. You're beautiful, curvy in all the right places, and you pot a mean black ball. And best of all, you were obviously after a holiday fling. But it just didn't feel right."

She opened her arms wide. "Come here."

I had no hesitation as I set down my cup and moved into her arms. And we simply held each other with no thought of sex, no ulterior motive, just the comfort of friends. For that was what we were.

"Will we ever get over our exes?" I asked her.

Her sigh stirred my hair. "I hope so. Have to. I can't see myself staying celibate forever, and this masturbation thing is getting old already. I've got my fingers diddled off."

"So no little toys snuck into your baggage at all?"

"I already told you—too scared of customs. I could picture them dragging me aside for a security screen and going through my bags, through my ratty underwear and T-shirts, and pulling out my vibrator, holding it aloft for all to see, and saying in a loud voice, 'So this is what set off the alarm. You can go now, Ms. Kratzmann.'"

I laughed. "Nearly as bad as when my mam found my first vibrator. It was one of those little purse things, a pocket rocket. More of a clit buzzer really. She didn't know what it was. She came down to breakfast with it and said to my *entire* family, 'I found your alarm clock under your pillow, Nora, but I think it's broken. The alarm doesn't work; it only buzzes.'"

There was a beat of silence, and then Moni and I were laughing, a companionable laugh, deep and hearty.

I was comfortable with Moni, and now that we understood each other, where we were both coming from, a germ of an idea crept into my head. I moved away from her, stood, and went over to the armchair on the other side of the room. I sat with my legs spread and hoicked my T-shirt up to reveal my knickers. She watched me with wide eyes.

"Do you trust me?" I asked. "This is for me, but it could also be for both of us." When she nodded, I dipped my hand down underneath the waistband of my knickers. My fingers worked a familiar path down through my bush to settle in my favorite configuration—three fingers lightly tickling my pussy lips.

"The last time Ger and I made love," I started, "it was the hot and desperate kind. She ripped the button off my jeans trying to get my pants undone. Then she had me on my back on the bed with three fingers inside me." I closed my eyes remembering. There was the pain of knowing it wouldn't be repeated ever again, but the memory stirred an excitement and longing that I hadn't felt since.

My fingers started to stroke a familiar pattern, around and over my pussy lips in light touches. I was wet thinking of Ger, wet in a way that I hadn't been last night when Moni was kissing me. I remembered Ger's eyes, green like a cat's, like the faeries, and her small fingers pushing inside me. I remembered her voice. "*Come for me, Nora. Come for me.*"

"What happened then?" Moni's voice wafted across the room.

I opened my eyes to see her propped against the headboard. Her legs were bent, spread wide apart, and she had her fingers between them. Unlike me, she had removed her knickers, and I could see her bush, as blond as her head and so fine and pale that at first I thought she'd shaved. One finger was circling her clit in a slow, slow movement.

My fingers moved faster, and when I closed my eyes again, I could see Ger in my mind. "She fucked me with three fingers," I said. "She has small fingers, but she knows how to use them. I was wet, so very wet, and although we'd had almost no foreplay, I wanted her so much that when she pushed her fingers inside me I nearly came on the spot."

"Show me what she did." Moni's voice was low, husky.

My eyes locked with hers. "Like this." I tried to push three fingers inside myself, but my knickers made it impossible. Impatiently, I worked them over my hips, kicked them aside. Moni's gaze on my cunt added to the scene. I knew she wouldn't touch me, wouldn't come over here, we'd already established that trust. And besides, neither of us wanted it. But this... This was something we could share.

I couldn't get the angle exactly right of course, but I think she got the idea. I pushed three fingers up inside and started to fuck myself. My fingers were longer than Ger's, and it wasn't the same, it couldn't be the same, but I closed my eyes and pretended they were Ger's fingers inside me.

"Did you come when she fucked you?" Moni's voice floated across the room, a part of this scenario, but also outside it, separate.

"Yes." I was close to coming now. Ger in my head, and Moni across the room pushed me closer to the edge.

Moni's legs were now spread wide and straight like a doll on a mantelpiece. But no doll I'd ever seen had a blond muff like hers, or fingers that flickered and circled around her clit. When she used two fingers to spread herself wide so that I could see her pink clit, hard and protruding, surrounded by puffy lips, I nearly lost it. For a moment, I badly wanted to touch her, to lie between her legs and suck that prominent clit into my mouth until she came and came again. She was slick, wet with passion, and very beautiful. I pulled my fingers from my own pussy, and my muscles tensed. I would stand up and, ignoring the throbbing between my own legs, settle myself between her thighs. I would lick her until she came. I would fuck her until she came again. And she would do the same for me and drive the hovering ghost of Geraldine out of my head.

My hands came down on the arms of the chair, ready to rise, but a sound stopped me.

"Em," she moaned. "Oh Em, darling."

Her eyes were closed and her knees bent as she drove her fingers deep within herself. Her head tilted forward, her hair fell over her face, and her entire body shuddered as she came hard.

The moment passed, and I was glad. This wasn't about me and Moni; this was about me and Ger, and Moni and the unknown Em. Moni was still bent forward as she relaxed down after her climax. She hadn't seen my hesitation or how close I'd come to changing our unspoken bargain.

My hand settled down between my legs again, and I brought Ger's face back into my mind. Her full breasts, so firm and plump, her flat belly and flaring, womanly hips. And of course that patch of fire between her thighs.

I was conscious of finishing the show for Moni as she had done for me, so I spread myself as she had done, and scissored my clit between two fingers. The sideways pressure, a slow squeeze and release never failed to bring me off. This morning was no exception. The orgasm crashed over me in a wave of white light, of lightheadedness and throbbing glory between my legs.

When I relaxed, I saw Moni opposite me, her T-shirt pulled down to a decent level. Conscious of my disheveled state, I did the same, and I stood on suddenly wobbly legs.

"Bathroom," I muttered through a tight throat and disappeared into the small room.

When I came out, Moni was tidying the room, plumping up the pillows, and straightening the duvet.

"I'm sure they have room service," I said, and my voice was back to normal.

She flashed me a grin. "I'm sure they do, but it's no trouble to do this."

As I gathered my clothes, I noticed I'd left a small wet spot on the upholstered chair. I wasn't sure what to do. This wasn't like the morning after with a lover; it wasn't exactly a friends-only situation either. Moni had no such qualms. She came over and rose onto her tiptoes to kiss me on the lips. It wasn't a lover's kiss, more a casual friend's kiss.

"Would you like first shower?" she asked. "There's towels and soap and stuff in the bathroom."

I nodded, and the normality of her remark restored the balance between us. The vague overlay of lovers vanished.

"Would you like to go for breakfast?" I asked. "I know a great place not far from here that does brilliant French toast with strawberries."

"Oh yes!" Her response was instantaneous. "I'm starving!"

I showered quickly and dressed in last night's clothes. While Moni was in the shower, I checked my mobile. Nothing from Ger, although by now I was expecting the absence. There was a text from Sue, asking if I fancied doing something today. Something touristy, she said.

With a glance at the bathroom door, I texted Sue that I'd love to and would she like to come for breakfast at the Egg and Spoon, and we could work it out from there.

Moni emerged from the bathroom toweling her hair. I was most impressed she didn't bother with a hairdryer. She seemed the type to spend hours fluffing and primping in front of a mirror, but she looked relaxed and casual in jeans and a sky blue T-shirt.

"Your last full day in London," I said. "Do you have plans?"

"Ever since I was a kid, I've wanted to go to the Tower of London."

"Do you fancy company? My friend Sue—my *straight* friend Sue—is going to meet us for breakfast. She wants to do something touristy today; she's Australian, and although she's been here for a few years, she's been working too hard to see many of the sights."

"I'm up for that. Be good to have the company."

CHAPTER 12

SUE WAS WAITING AT THE Egg and Spoon when we arrived. I hadn't mentioned that I was bringing someone, but she was the picture of restraint even though she was obviously dying to know about Moni. At least for the first five minutes. I introduced them, they made a few polite remarks, and we sat and studied the menus.

"The Big Breakfast for me," said Sue. "Order for me, will you? I'm bursting for a pee." She disappeared in the direction of the loos at the back.

Moni, who was sitting next to me, stared after her. "She's real cute."

"She's real straight too."

"Yeah, you said. No more straight women for me."

I'd never heard Sue called "cute" before. She was one of those rangy, raw-boned women who were normally called handsome or attractive. Never beautiful or cute.

Sue must have flushed her tactful gene down the toilet, as when she returned she launched straight into it. "So, how did you two meet? I'm a bit surprised—no offence, Moni—but our Nora's been pining lately. I didn't expect her to climb back on the train so quickly."

Moni laughed. "We're friends. We don't have anything going. I'm free and available if you're interested."

I groaned. "No straight women, remember?"

Opposite me, Sue blinked slowly as if surprised by the proposition, although she was used to being hit on by women when she came with me to the dyke bars.

"Yeah, you're right. Sorry, Sue, but I'm heading for Paris tomorrow anyway."

Sue flapped a hand. "No worries. But call me first next time, eh? Don't waste your time with Nora."

I swallowed my surprise. Sue had *never* offered a would-be suitor any kind of encouragement when someone tried to pick her up.

The waitress came, and we accepted coffee and ordered breakfast. After she departed, Sue leaned across the table. "You're friends?" She nailed me with her gaze. "Really? You can tell your Auntie Sue."

"Friends," I repeated. I pushed down the image of Moni sitting opposite me with her fingers in her pussy.

Sue settled back in her chair and directed her next remark at Moni. "She told you about Ger?"

"She did." Moni sipped her coffee, set it back on the table, and added more milk. "Which is why we're friends and not lovers."

Sue seemed to buy it. "Pity. I'd have liked my friend to stop pining and move on with her life. Find someone new."

I glared at her. "Pot. Kettle."

Moni glanced from Sue to me and back again. "I think there's a bit going on here that I don't know about."

Luckily our breakfast arrived before she could pursue it, and the next few minutes were taken up with "pass the salt" and "do they have Tabasco here?" and "I'm dying for more coffee" and then the steady sound of empty bellies being filled.

Sue wiped her mouth with her napkin and sat back. "I'm stuffed. Good fuel for all the tourist things today. So where shall we go?" Her look encompassed Moni.

"Moni's only got one day left, and she really wants to see the Tower of London."

"Sounds good," said Sue. "I've never done that either."

We took the tube to the Tower Hill, deciding to head straight there in case there were queues. There were long ones, and an usher told us we should have booked ahead. But he took pity on Moni with only a day in London and quietly shepherded us into a priority line.

The Tower was spectacular, and the Crown Jewels amazing. Even Sue, who had strong views on the monarchy and especially their role in Australia, was impressed, although she shot off a few acerbic comments about the unnecessary nature of extreme wealth. We took the obligatory photos of ravens, posed with Beefeaters, and ruled against the overpriced coffee shop crowded with kids, deciding to find a pub instead.

Moni surprised us by ordering a pint of Guinness, so we both felt obliged to join her, but the stiff, cold wind from the Thames quickly sobered us up once we left the pub.

"I'm going to head away," Moni said. "I've got a ticket to see *Cats*, and then if I've got any energy, I'm going to find a nightclub. You're both welcome to join me there."

"Not me," I said. "I'm for an early night."

"Me neither," said Sue. "I'm meeting a friend later."

We both hugged Moni and exchanged e-mail addresses with a promise to get in touch if we were ever in Dallas. She kissed me on the lips and squeezed my hand. "Thank you," she whispered in my ear.

Then she kissed Sue, also on the lips, and I'm sure it wasn't my imagination that the kiss lingered longer than mine.

Sue had a strange look on her face as she stared after Moni's departing back.

"You okay?" I asked. "Guinness not agreeing with you?"

Sue shook herself like a terrier. "I'm fine. Are you heading home? I'm meeting Ash in Camberwell, so I'm going your way."

We were quiet as we boarded the tube. I looked across at Sue; she had her head back and her eyes closed. I wondered what she was thinking about.

"Fancy a coffee?" she asked as we exited the station. "I've got time."

I nodded in agreement, and we went to my place as it was close. Tomás greeted us noisily at the door—Sue was a favorite of his—and she hauled him up for a snuggle while I put the coffee on.

"Leo called me last night," she said, her face buried in Tomás's fur. "I told him to go fuck himself."

I studied her. Sue was the kind of person who would smile when the world ended, and she'd given no sign of heartbreak during the day with Moni.

"How do you feel?" I asked cautiously.

She lifted her face from Tomás. "Fine," she said. "Fucking great actually. It's a relief not to care. I think I may be over the hump of heartbreak."

After that, we chatted about inconsequential things, like work and TV programs—all the normal chatter between friends.

The time with Moni had shown me two things. First, I wasn't yet ready to move on from Ger, but at some time in the future that day *would* come. It was hard to think of that day. Ger was still so much a part of my life—in my heart if not in my bed. A couple of times when waking from dreams, I caught myself stretching a hand out for her in bed. The pain when I remembered she wasn't there was as sharp as ever.

I decided to carry on living my life as best I could—work, the dyke bar for pool—but no pickups—breakfast with my family once a week, and time with Sue and other friends. Life moved on through the foggy London autumn and into the sharpness of winter. I turned the heating up in my flat and made more of an effort on the interior decor, but the memory of Ger's effortless good taste put my paltry efforts to shame. I settled for a couple of fringed gypsy shawls draped over the sofa and some bright red kitchen accessories. I spent more time cooking at home and started inviting more friends around for dinner. There were some riotous evenings over good food, cheap wine, and great conversation. And through it all, I missed Geraldine.

Instead of getting easier, it became harder. She'd be in my head for the smallest of reasons. How she'd set her lips to the same place on the glass as mine. How she'd tucked her hand in my pocket as we'd walked to my flat. I'd see someone with her height and build or with her hair, and my heart would leap in anticipation. But it was never her.

And throughout the chilly days late in the year, I remembered my sister Mary's words often. "You'll know when it happens to you." I'd scoffed at the thought. But now, even as I pretended I was enjoying myself, there was a space inside my heart that belonged to Ger. An ache of longing that wouldn't go away.

If this was love, I didn't want it.

But as the days moved past, one after the other, piling into a morass of work and empty space and attempts at fun, I realized Mary was right. Love did arrive with a thump, and for better or worse, I loved Ger.

CHAPTER 13

THEN, ONE DAY ON THE downslide to Christmas, I bumped into her. It was inevitable, I suppose. After all, two dykes in London would naturally frequent some of the same places. But I bumped into her at the Camden Lock Market, far from my usual haunts. I was with Sue, wandering around in a halfhearted attempt to buy presents for my family. Sue was my barometer of…well, not good taste, but at least she steered me away from the woefully bad. I was browsing a stall of knick-knacks, looking for something for Mam, when a voice next to me said, "Hello, Nora."

It was Geraldine. My fingers froze on the silver teaspoons I was looking at. I slowly turned my head, and she was there at my side. She was paler and looked tired. Her glorious hair was bundled on top of her head, half covered by a Rasta hat and despite being bundled up in a Paddington Bear duffle coat, I could see she'd lost weight. There were hollows in her cheeks and dark shadows under her eyes.

I put the teaspoons down and turned to face her. I didn't know what to say. I'd fantasized about coming face- to- face with her for months, but now that the moment was here, I didn't know how to treat it.

"How have you been?" I asked finally.

She gave a half shake of her head, and a long curl of hair tumbled free from the hat. "Fine. You?"

I started to say "fine" but Sue appeared at my elbow, an avenging warrior out to protect me.

"Don't you dare say 'fine' Nora." She turned to Ger. "I'm Nora's friend, Sue, and I know you're Geraldine. Would you like to have coffee first, or shall I disembowel you now and save myself three quid?"

"Sue, please," I started to say, but Sue cut me off with a wave of her hand.

"Don't worry," she said. "I'll say my piece and leave you to it." She turned to Ger, and her eyes softened. Ger looked shell-shocked and fragile, as if Sue's words might pound her into the ground. "I'm sorry to be harsh," Sue said. "But you're breaking Nora's heart. Nora's my friend, and I hate to see her suffering. She loves you; do you get that? Love, not lust, not anything halfhearted, but *love*. From what she's said, you care for her too. And you're throwing it away on a stupid family feud that's gone on since the dark ages, and no one can remember exactly why anymore." She touched Ger's hand. "Think about it." And then to me, "I'll be over there if you need me." She disappeared and left me alone with Ger and a few hundred milling people.

"She's something, your friend," Ger said, and her voice was nearly back to normal, as if Sue's forceful words had opened her throat.

"She is." I didn't want to talk about Sue. I wanted to look at Ger, wanted to see if we could fix what we had broken. "Do you want to get a coffee?"

She hesitated. "Nothing's changed, Nora. I can't do it. I can't choose you over my family."

"You can't know that's what would happen."

"I can. My brother Pádraig mentioned seeing your brother Brian at a football match, and my dad went ape. Asked Pádraig why he didn't beat Brian to a pulp...said he'd have got away with it in the crowd."

"What did Pádraig say?"

"Nothing much. He's pretty peaceful. He just said he didn't see the point, and Dad said, 'Don't you forget there is a point. You must never forget.'" She shook her head again. "I'm sorry, Nora. I just can't. My family means too much to me."

"And me?" My mouth was dry with the urgency of convincing her. As if this was the only chance I would have again. "What am I? Chopped liver?"

She raised a small smile. "No, never that. Chopped sirloin at least." She turned away. "I shouldn't have said hello. I don't know what I was thinking. I guess I just wanted to see you for a minute, see how you're doing. I'll go. I'm making it worse."

"Wait." I stopped her with a hand on her arm. "Sue's right. I haven't gotten over you. I love you, Ger, and I am willing to give up my family for you if it comes to it. We had something that I don't think either of us will find again. I know it was only a few nights, but it doesn't take a lifetime to build love. Sometimes it just emerges, like a butterfly from a cocoon. That's what it was like. But now that butterfly can't go back to being a caterpillar."

"I'm sorry, Nora." She turned away, and my hand fell from her arm.

"Can I see you again?" I called after her. "Lunch? Coffee?"

But she was gone, swallowed up by the crowds. I looked for her bright hair under that ridiculous hat and the Air Force blue duffel coat, but she'd vanished.

I slumped against the stall and earned a frown from the stall holder. I looked around for Sue. She was already approaching like a ship in full sail. She didn't need to ask me how it went; one look at my face said it all. Grabbing my arm she steered me through the crowds to a pub, pushed me into a seat, and went to the bar only to return with a double brandy.

"Drink this," she said, thrusting it at me.

"I don't like brandy," I started to say, but one look at her fierce face persuaded me it was easier to drink it.

The brandy forged a warm and glowing path to my stomach.

Sue sighed. "You don't need to tell me what she said. I can read it all from your body language."

I nodded. But the encounter told me one thing; Ger still cared. No one could be as fragile as she looked and be indifferent. She must feel something for me, and it showed in her weight loss, tired eyes, and the tentative nature of her voice. And if she still cared, then there was hope.

I went home to Mam and Da for a weekend rather than just a single morning. My eyes followed them around, considering. That stupid fecking feud. Did it still extend past my father's insistence, Theresa's sharp words, and Declan and his fists? Was it still alive? Was it? Brian was possibly the sanest and most rational of my brothers, my confidante from childhood. He was a year older than me, and we'd always been close. When we were in the pub, I asked his opinion.

"I think the feud's bollocks," he said. "But our parents don't. To them, there's as much hatred as ever. I see Pádraig Flannery sometimes in passing. We're cordial, no more beating each other up. But I avoid his brother, Young Seánie. He'd take me down as soon as look at me, and it's got worse since he had that run in with Declan and Theresa a couple of months back.

Part of it, I think, is that he was bested by a girl, even if she didn't mean to push him under a car."

"What do you think would happen, metaphorically speaking of course, if I were to date a Flannery?"

Brian peered into my face. "Is this why you've been moping? Oh, Nora..." The noise of the pub swelled around us. "Which one?"

"Geraldine."

His brow furrowed. "Skinny kid with red plaits?"

"Didn't they all look like that? Especially the boys." The joke fell flat.

Brian propped his chin on his hand and stared at me, pint forgotten. "They'd kill you. And when they'd finished killing you, they'd go out and start a brawl with any Flannery they could find."

"You think so?" I started ripping tiny shreds from a beer mat.

"I know so." He covered my hand, momentarily stilling my fingers beneath his strong, protective hand. "It's not just Declan, Theresa, and Young Seánie, who are the hotheads in the families. Any time the feud looks like dying down, someone stirs it up again. Remember when Rose Flannery was on the track team with our Mary and was paired with her for training? Mary and Rose were managing—the important thing to them was running—but Da went stomping and swearing to the athletics club and got it changed. And then came home and blasted Mary for thinking it was all right. That wasn't so long ago."

"Three years. What's three years in a feud that's already lasted for generations?" I ripped a long shred from the beer mat with a fierce movement.

Brian nodded. "But it's about time this stupid feud came to an end. If you have the guts to do it...if Geraldine does...I'll back you all the way. But you risk losing the family. Not me. Never me. But I can't speak for the others. Is she worth it, Nora?"

My eyes fixed on the shreds of cardboard that used to be a beer mat. "She is."

"Then go get your woman."

CHAPTER 14

It wasn't easy. But I had a campaign mapped out in my head, and this time I wasn't going to be put off.

I called her, but she never picked up. It meant I heard her voice on the voicemail, but she never returned my calls.

I went back to the pub where we'd first met, and there were many beautiful women there, but they weren't my Geraldine.

Next I tracked down her work. She'd never told me exactly where she worked, but I rang every firm of architects within a ten-mile radius, asking for her until I got a positive response. I made an appointment to see her under a false name, but when I arrived, the receptionist took one look at me.

"Please take a seat," she said.

Rather than picking up the phone to tell Ger her client was waiting, she disappeared. I could hear the click clack of her heels fading down the corridor, then after a short pause, she returned. "I'm sorry," she said. "Ms. Flannery is unavailable."

"I can wait." I crossed one leg over the other and picked up a *Home Beautiful* magazine.

The receptionist fidgeted. "I'm sorry, Ms. Kelly, but she knows it's you regardless of the name you gave. She doesn't want to see you. I must ask you to leave." She moved to the door and held it open.

I knew when I was beaten. Holding my head high, I thanked the red-faced receptionist and left. I tried waiting outside Ger's office building, but she never appeared. She must have left by another door.

I had one hope left.

That Friday night, I left another message on Ger's mobile. "I love you, Ger, and I'm not giving up. I'm not going to let our families stand in the way of our happiness. I'm going to visit your parents on the weekend."

There was no response. I think she thought—hoped—I wasn't brave enough to do it.

I went home on Saturday night. If I were going to lose my family, then I would enjoy one last happy time with them before they disowned me. For, regardless of the outcome, they would know I had gone to see the Flannerys, and that alone was a hanging offence in our home. I went to the pub with Da, Brian, Mary, and Mary's boyfriend Liam, who was still ensconced in Mary's life. There was Irish music that raised the rafters, and I drank enough to lose my inhibitions and dance a jig with Mary. We clasped hands and high-stepped and leaped until we were both breathless.

Brian watched me as he played the bodhrán in the session. I could see the worry in his eyes even from across the room.

On Sunday morning, I told my family I was going for a walk. If they thought it strange I was dressed neatly in my best black jeans and a respectable jacket over a pale yellow shirt, they didn't say anything. They just nodded and returned to the eggs and rashers. I went around the table, kissing everyone on the top of the head saying, "Love you Mam, love you Da, love you sis," until they were all squirming.

Brian was waiting at the front door. Like me, he was dressed tidier than I'd expect for a family breakfast. "I'm coming with you."

Tears sprang to my eyes at his show of support, and I linked my arm through his.

"Don't you think you should have worn a darker shirt?" he asked. "It will be murder getting the blood out of that."

I knew the way to the Flannery family home. Like us, they lived in a terrace, tidy and orderly. I knocked on the door. Footsteps clumped down the passageway, and the door swung open. Pádraig Flannery stood there; a big hulking side of a man, but a reasonable one according to Brian.

I lifted my chin. "I'm here to see Geraldine."

Pádraig gave me a slow look from the top of my head down to my black boots. Then he glanced at Brian. "You in this, Kelly?" he asked. "You know this isn't a good idea."

"It's Nora's idea," Brian replied. "And I think it's about time."

Pádraig returned his heavy gaze to me. "We're eating breakfast. I'll see if she'll come out."

"No." I drew myself up to the full five feet eight. "I'm coming in. What needs to be said needs to be said to all of you." I pushed past him into the hall before he could react and followed my nose. These houses were all alike; the kitchen would be at the back.

The kitchen was bigger than ours, lit with the weak sunlight that came in via great French doors to the garden. The Flannery family was all there, and I mentally ticked off each name as I looked around the table—the parents, Seán and Frances, Young Seánie, Ruth, Rose, Fergal, a space for Pádraig who was standing behind me, breathing down my neck. And Geraldine. Geraldine's fork clattered to her plate when I walked in. Her sudden pallor told me that, despite my text message, she wasn't expecting this.

I fixed my gaze on her parents. "Good morning. I apologize for barging in on you all like this, but what I have to say can't wait. My name is Nora Kelly and this is my brother Brian. I—"

My speech wasn't prepared; it just came out of my mouth, but it was cut off by a roar as Seán Flannery lumbered to his feet. His hand came down on the table with a crash, and the sauce bottle went flying. "I know who you are. No Kelly is welcome in my house. Get out now before I throw you out."

Young Seánie and Fergal also rose to their feet and moved to stand shoulder to shoulder with their father. With an apologetic glance at Brian, Pádraig moved to join them.

I daren't look at Geraldine. "Please Mr. Flannery, just hear me out. This won't take long." I took a deep breath. "My parents don't know I'm here, and I'm sure when they hear of it, they will react just as you are. They'll probably throw me out of their house simply for talking to you. And then there's Geraldine."

"What about her?" Antagonism rolled off him in waves, but at least I was still in the house. At least he was still listening.

"I love her. And I think she loves me. But this feud between our families is ruining our chance at happiness. Geraldine refused to see me once she found out I was a Kelly."

"As she should." He folded his arms across his chest, and next to him, Young Seánie looked poised to manhandle me to the door.

"With due respect, isn't it time this ended? What our grandparents did is long past. There are enough barriers to love these days." I glanced at Geraldine. Her gaze drilled my face, and she was whiter than sun-bleached sheets. "Especially our sort of love."

I swiveled to appeal to Geraldine's mother. "Mrs. Flannery, don't you want your daughter to be happy?"

Frances Flannery also folded her arms. "She'll find someone. Someone who isn't a lying, cheating, black-hearted Kelly."

I sensed my time had run out; their ears were already closed against me. But I had to make one last attempt. "What happened between our families was over sixty years ago. Does it still matter? All this hate is hard to sustain."

It was the wrong thing to say. Seán Kelly's hands closed into fists, and he took a step forward. I thought he was going to punch me, but I stood my ground. Brian took a step closer to me, and his hands came up to the ready position.

Seán's eyes narrowed, and he seemed to be weighing where to land the first punch. "You can make light of it, but sixty years is nothing but a spit in the passing of time. You're wrong, lassie. It does matter, and hate is the easiest thing to sustain. Now get out of my house before I forget my manners and throw you out."

Failure sat thickly in my throat. I turned to go, and as I did, I saw Geraldine sitting like a statue at the table. Her sisters stared at their plates as if wishing this were over so they could resume their breakfast. But Geraldine... She was staring at me. Her eyes shimmered bright, and there was a tension in her body.

I stared at her, willing her to come to me. "I love you, Geraldine. That will never change. You know where to find me if you want to."

I turned on my heel, stuck my chin up, and forced myself to saunter down the hall to the front door, Brian at my back. Pádraig followed Brian. I didn't look back, but I heard Brian's curt acknowledgement of thanks, and Pádraig's slow rumbling reply.

Tears blurred my vision. There was nothing left now. I must walk away, back to my flat, as my own family wouldn't want anything to do with me now that I'd made an appeal to the enemy. For a brief and fierce moment, I hated them. It took two sides to make a feud, and my family was as bad as the Flannerys. Frances Flannery was right—I didn't know exactly what had gone down in the past, so it wasn't my place to call for forgiveness. It was easy to hate.

But it was also easy to love. And the past didn't belong to Geraldine and me.

Brian paced by my side, and I was grateful for his silence. He would cop it when he got home, but he'd be all right. It wasn't his battle, and he had only been standing up for me.

"Nora! Wait!"

The shout came down the street, uneven with the sound of running feet. I slowed, and the runner caught up with me. Geraldine was out of breath, and her shirt had come untucked from her jeans in her haste. Her bright hair was disheveled.

She had been crying, and there were red marks around her wrists. Despite logic, a flare of hope lit my heart. I waited for her to speak.

She was out of breath. "You're brave, Nora. Not like me. You tried to change things. I just accepted them." She rubbed the red mark on one wrist. "They tried to stop me following you. I elbowed Young Seánie in the guts. I don't think he'll care if I don't return."

She stepped closer, and I longed to reach out and gather her into my arms. But I had to be sure what she was saying. This still could be the last hurrah.

"I'm coming with you. If you still want me. If you'll have me."

Beside me, Brian sucked a breath and took a pace or two away. Near enough to be there if I needed him, far enough to give us a bit of privacy.

"For how long, Geraldine? Until your mam comes calling, begging for you to come home?"

"I'll marry you, if you'll have me. Is that long enough?"

"And your family?"

She shrugged, but I could see her pain. "I choose you. As you have chosen me."

Still I hesitated. I had to be sure. I couldn't take her back only for her to stomp all over my heart again.

"No more family breakfasts. No more weekends at home in your childhood bed. No more Frances to sit and chat with over a cup of tea."

She was crying now, the tears streaming in silent tracks down her cheeks. "I choose you."

It was enough. I stepped forward, so did she, and when we met, our arms went around each other forming a circle of our own, a bond that couldn't be broken. It wasn't family, but it was enough. It was more. She raised her mouth for my kiss, and I kissed her as if I were drowning. The salt of our tears mingled on our cheeks, touched our lips.

"Come home with me," I said and linked our hands together. We started down the road into our life together.

Brian left us at the corner to head back to Mam and Da's. "I won't tell them," he said. "But you can be sure they'll find out."

I nodded. Nothing to do there. I just had to wait and see which way the cards fell.

Ger and I went to my flat. On the train we sat close together, not talking, but with our hands entwined. There would be talking later, that was certain, but right now I savored her nearness, the touch of her hands in mine, and the rightness of sitting so close together. We walked into my flat to be greeted by a pissed off Tomás and the smell of dirty cat litter. I topped up his food bowl in apology for my absence, dealt with the cat litter, and then turned back to Ger.

"I've been wanting this. You, here with me again."

"I'm sorry," she said. "I'm so sorry I left you. I shouldn't have. When Young Seánie tried to stop me following you, that's when I knew they would have to come to me if they wanted to see me again."

I glanced at the clock; only eleven. So much had happened in a scant few hours.

I turned to Ger. "What do you want to do?"

"Kiss you," she said. "Make love to you."

"Now?"

She smiled and touched my cheek. "Can you think of a better time?"

I couldn't.

I let her lead me to my bedroom and shut the door against a startled Tomás. The last time Ger and I had been together, she'd ripped my clothes off with a desperation I hadn't understood. This time, the urgency was muted. We came to a halt in the middle of the floor. My bed wasn't made, and I moved to fix it, but she touched my hand.

"Leave it. It's not important."

So I settled for sweeping the duvet onto the floor.

She came to me then and lifted her arms to wind them around my neck. We moved together—thigh to thigh, belly to belly, breast to breast. She lifted her mouth for my kiss, and the moment hung in the air between us.

I will remember this, I thought. Not our first kiss, but our first kiss when I knew for sure we had a future together. And then Ger kissed me, and all coherent thought left my head. She kissed me sweet and deep, long kisses that spun me out of time. There were sparks behind my eyes, and if the room was spinning, it was because Ger, the center of my universe, was so still and strong.

When kissing wasn't enough, I undressed her—slipped her jacket from her shoulders, traced the neckline of her shirt, and then ran a finger down to her cleavage. Her skin was soft, shivery where I touched her, and her eyes were fever-bright. She wore a black bra under her shirt, with opaque satin cups. Nothing fancy, just chain store underwear, but on her it was as beautiful as if it were French lace. I left it in place while I unfastened her jeans and pushed them down over her hips. Her knickers were cotton, and they didn't match her bra, but that made it all the more real. She'd dressed for herself that morning, not for a lover.

When I had her down to only underwear, she undressed me with just as much care. I'd dressed smartly to the skin that morning for confidence, and my cream-colored bra matched my knickers, and both were new.

"Confident?" she teased as she embraced me and undid the snap with a deft flick.

"No," I answered. "It was armor for when I was thrown out on the street by your family."

Her eyes were somber for a moment, and I kicked myself for reminding her. But then she slid her hands around my neck once more.

"It's you and me now, Nora."

The words glowed in my heart. I wanted to wrap them carefully, make them a memory. *You and me*. They echoed in my head. It was Ger and me. Geraldine and Nora.

"I can't think of anything better," I said.

And then the time for talking was past, and I drew her to the bed. We shed the rest of our clothes—my new and matching underwear, her mismatched old set—and we lay naked on the cotton sheets with the weak and wintry sunlight filtering through the window to haze our skin with a soft glow.

We kissed for long moments, relearning the shape and the taste of each other, before I allowed my hands to cup her generous breasts and my fingertips to flutter over her nipples. The air in the room was cool enough that they were peaking anyway, but they hardened further under my touch. I tasted her breasts, pressed kisses to their upper slope, and took first one, then the other nipple in my mouth and sucked her with lazy appreciation. Ger's hands pushed into my hair and held me there as she encouraged me with breathy gasps and words of love.

She wasn't passive either. Even as I explored the under curve of her breasts and smoothed her belly, her fingers traced my nipples and mapped patterns on my back. Her fingers dipped between my thighs while I was still feathering through her luxuriant patch. I hadn't clipped my pubes since she'd left, and my bush was denser, softer than it had been for a long time.

"I like it," she mumbled and rolled so she half covered me. She put her mouth to my breast, two fingers in my cunt, and brushed my clit with her thumb. I was wet and open for her, and the touch of her thumb pushed me closer to the precipice.

I'd wanted to make it good for her, give her pleasure before my own, but her fingers and mouth were doing such magic I couldn't find the words to stop her. My hands pressed into the sheets at my sides, unwilling to constrain her if it meant she'd stop. She withdrew her fingers, and started slow, tortuous circles around my clit. She alternated those soft strokes with two fingers slipping in and out of me. The world turned red and hazy behind my eyes, and the low ache of anticipation built in my belly. I came hard with great shuddering racks of pleasure, spasming around her fingers.

She held me through the aftershocks, kissing my face, my lips.

"Tell me what you want," I said when I could speak again. "Tell me what you dreamed of while we were apart."

She looked at me with hooded eyes, wicked and anticipatory.

"Your mouth," she said. "Your mouth between my legs and your tongue on my pussy."

I moved along her body until I was nestled between her thighs, my face near her cunt. Her musky smell enticed me and drew me in.

I teased her with the point of my tongue, moving around her lips, avoiding her jutting clit, and tasting her. Her thighs twitched restlessly, her buttocks clenched as the pleasure grew. Still I teased, continuing to avoid the center of her pleasure and concentrating on enjoying the whole of her. But I couldn't take it when she started to beg—we'd had enough begging in our relationship already. So I put my mouth over her clit and sucked and lapped and licked and made circles with my tongue until she came hard against my mouth. Her cries filled the bedroom with her joy.

Afterwards, we held each other—her head on my shoulder, her hand cupping my breast, mine stroking her side. We lay and talked until the sun filled the room in the early afternoon and Tomás's scratching at the bedroom door grew more desperate. Then we let him in, and he curled up by Geraldine's side and purred in contentment.

We rose, dressed, and went for a walk around the neighborhood hand in hand, wandering like any couple in love. Eschewing the pubs for our own company, we bought a bottle of wine and some sushi and sat in the park until it was too cool and damp to stay longer. Then we went back to my flat to plan our future together.

EPILOGUE

OF COURSE IT WASN'T SMOOTH sailing at first. We bought a flat together, larger than her studio but furnished as beautifully by Ger's good taste. Our friends visited—particularly Sue whose break with Leo proved final. At first Brian was our only family visitor, but one day I opened the door to find Pádraig on the step.

Ger and I married a year after we got back together. Brian and Pádraig came to the ceremony, and my sister, Mary, and Ger's sister, Rose, stood up beside us. I caught a fleeting glimpse of Frances Flannery at the back of the registry office, but she was gone before either of us could acknowledge her.

The tension eased softly, stealthily—a chink here, a gap there. Now, two years later it's nearly all okay. Our parents talk to us. Brian is dating Ger's sister, Ruth. Our fathers have arrived at the stage of nodding at each other in cordial acknowledgement. Prickly and uncertain, but it's a start. Our mothers do better, as mothers always do. Mam dropped the fact that she'd had coffee with Frances Flannery the other day. Just the two of them.

And Ger and me? We're happy. When we lie in bed at night with her head on my shoulder and her hair tickling my nose, we look out at the lights of London, our city, and I'm happy.

Her smile turns my heart when I hand her the first coffee of the day through the shower door. Quite simply, we love each other above all else.

And that's the way it's going to be from now on.

NOT-SO-STRAIGHT SUE

by Cheyenne Blue

THE LONG LONDON EVENING WAS sliding into darkness when we left the pub. It was a couple of miles to my flat, but I decided to walk. I wanted to think about what had rolled out of my mouth. Going back to Oz. I hadn't given any thought to that idea before this evening.

It would be easy to dismiss it as a maudlin bout of homesickness brought about by too much wine. I'd had the pangs of longing for a wide flat vista and a well-trodden veranda before, but they were just that—pangs. They lasted no longer than a couple of minutes and a chorus of *Waltzing Matilda*. Even now, as I paced the busy street, dodging the giggling gangs of girls, I still had a longing to be somewhere else. Somewhere quieter. Somewhere I belonged.

Deliberately, I set my thoughts to those things about home that were less than pleasurable. I thought of the drunken heckling at closing time of any woman under fifty. The absence of arts and entertainment that I so loved here in London—there were no galleries, café culture, or music events within 500 kilometers of Yeringup. Sure, the major cities had an abundance of culture, but those cities were two days' drive, and there was no budget airline to fly me there for $5, BYO sandwich, and dunny roll.

I thought of the insular community, the conservative values that still held sway. Ah yes, those bloody values. My thoughts skittered away from *that*. I wasn't yet ready to go there.

But matched up against the trials of life in a too-small town were the good things, which kept sneaking into my head like an old ABBA song and wouldn't be dislodged. A caring community where people looked out for each other. The feel of a good horse between your thighs. The excitement of polocrosse. Driving up a dusty road to home, knowing there was a cold beer in the fridge and a comfy couch for sitting. Taking too long to get the groceries because you'd had four conversations along the way with people you knew. A dog. A little ripper of a working dog by your side. I missed having a pup—it simply wasn't possible with my London lifestyle. Those things wound through my guts and pulled them tight until I was breathless with the longing for home.

I turned a corner into the busier street and increased my pace as I passed the takeaways, the pubs, and the convenience stores. London surrounded me with its noise, its ever-present hum, and people, always people. I'd loved living here. Loved it for all the things I didn't have in Queensland. But by the time I turned into my road and unlocked the door of my flat, my mind was made up. Like Frank-N-Furter from the *Rocky Horror Picture Show* blasting back to transsexual Transylvania, I was going home.

ABOUT CHEYENNE BLUE

Cheyenne Blue's fiction has been included in over ninety erotic anthologies since 2000, including *Best Lesbian Erotica*; *Best Women's Erotica*; *All You Can Eat: A Buffet of Lesbian Romance & Erotica*; *Sweat*; *Bossy*; and *Wild Girls, Wild Nights*. She is the editor of *Forbidden Fruit: stories of unwise lesbian desire*, a 2015 finalist for both the Lambda Literary Award and Golden Crown Literary Award, and of *First: Sensual Lesbian Stories of New Beginnings*.

Her collected lesbian short fiction is published as *Blue Woman Stories*, volumes 1-3, with more to come. Under her own name she has written travel books and articles and edited anthologies of local writing in Ireland. She has lived in the U.K., Ireland, the United States, and Switzerland, but now writes, runs, makes bread and cheese, and drinks wine by the beach in Queensland, Australia. Check out her blog at www.cheyenneblue.com and follow her on **Twitter** at @IamCheyenneBlue and on **Goodreads** at https://www. goodreads.com/CheyenneBlue.

OTHER BOOKS FROM
YLVA PUBLISHING

www.ylva-publishing.com

JUST PHYSICAL

Jae

ISBN: 978-3-95533-534-2
Length: 271 pages (116,000 words)

After being diagnosed with MS, actress Jill takes herself off the romantic market. On the set of a disaster movie, she meets stunt woman Crash, whose easy smile makes her wish things were different.

Despite their growing feelings, Jill is determined to let Crash into her bed, but not her heart. As they start to play with fire on and off camera, will they be able to keep things just physical?

BITTER FRUIT

Lois Cloarec Hart

ISBN: 978-3-95533-216-7
Length: 244 pages (50,000 words)

Jac accepts an unusual wager from her best friend. Jac has one month to seduce a young woman she's never met. Though Lauren is straight and engaged, Jac begins her campaign confident that she'll win the bet. But Jac's forgotten that if you sow an onion seed, you won't harvest a peach. When her plan goes awry, will she reap the bitter fruit of her deception? Or will Lauren turn the tables on her?

HEART'S SURRENDER

Emma Weimann

ISBN: 978-3-95533-183-2
Length: 305 pages (63,000 words)

Neither Samantha Freedman nor Gillian Jennings are looking for a relationship when they begin a no-strings-attached affair. But soon simple attraction turns into something more.

What happens when the worlds of a handywoman and a pampered housewife collide? Can nights of hot, erotic fun lead to love, or will these two very different women go their separate ways?

ALL THE LITTLE MOMENTS

G Benson

ISBN: 978-3-95533-341-6
Length: 350 pages (132,000 words)

Anna is focused on her career as an anaesthetist. When a tragic accident leaves her responsible for her young niece and nephew, her life changes abruptly. Completely overwhelmed, Anna barely has time to brush her teeth in the morning let alone date a woman. But then she collides with a long-legged stranger...

COMING FROM YLVA PUBLISHING

www.ylva-publishing.com

NOT-SO-STRAIGHT SUE
Cheyenne Blue

Lawyer Sue Brent has buried her queerness deep within, until a disastrous date forces her to confront the truth. She returns to her native Australia and an outback law practice. When Sue's friend, Moni, arrives to work as an outback doctor, Sue sees a new path to happiness with her. But Sue's first love, Denise, appears begging a favor, and Sue and Moni's burgeoning relationship is put to the test.

BUNNY FINDS A FRIEND
Hazel Yeats

Cara Jong's bad day doesn't improve after a run-in with Jude Donovan, who's playing Santa in a department store in Amsterdam. When Cara finds out that the woman beneath the Santa suit is a children's book writer, she's intrigued. But she doesn't trust her luck in love. Can Cara's meddling sisters and a hilarious road trip convince her to go after her happily-ever-after with the writer?

Never-Tied Nora
© 2015 by Cheyenne Blue

ISBN: 978-3-95533-451-2

Also available as e-book.

Published by Ylva Publishing, legal entity of Ylva Verlag, e.Kfr.

Ylva Verlag, e.Kfr.
Owner: Astrid Ohletz
Am Kirschgarten 2
65830 Kriftel
Germany

www.ylva-publishing.com

First edition: December 2015

Credits
Edited by Jove Belle
Proofread by Lannah Bernard
Cover Design & Printlayout by Streetlight Graphics

www.ingramcontent.com/pod-product-compliance
Lightning Source LLC
Chambersburg PA
CBHW022021170626
46808CB00003B/1016